Elizabeth pushed down on the gas pedal, desperate to get away from the crazy driver. But like an evil shadow, the truck clung to the back of the Jeep. As they whipped around a sharp curve, tires squealing, he hit her again. The Jeep swerved dangerously close to the edge of the cliff.

Horrified, Elizabeth struggled to maintain control of the Jeep. *Is he trying to run me off the road?* her mind screamed. The answer became obvious as the truck slammed her again.

"Hey, gorgeous!" the driver yelled to her. "Blow me a kiss!"

Elizabeth held her breath as she pushed the gas pedal down all the way. Terrified, she fishtailed around the next sharp curve, her tires screeching. Before she managed to straighten out the wheel, the crazy truck bumped her again from behind. Elizabeth's heart jumped into her throat as the Jeep swerved close to the edge of the cliff—close enough for her to catch a glimpse of the shimmering blue water far below.

Visit the Official Sweet Valley Web Site on the Internet at:

http://www.sweetvalley.com

FASHION VICTIM

Written by
Kate William

Created by
FRANCINE PASCAL

BANTAM BOOKS
NEW YORK · TORONTO · LONDON · SYDNEY · AUCKLAND

RL 6, age 12 and up

FASHION VICTIM

A Bantam Book / May 1997

Sweet Valley High®️ is a registered trademark of Francine Pascal.
Conceived by Francine Pascal.
Produced by Daniel Weiss Associates, Inc.
33 West 17th Street
New York, NY 10011.
Cover photography by Michael Segal.

ISBN: 0-553-57065-X

Published simultaneously in the United States and Canada

Bantam Books are published by Bantam Books, a division of Bantam Doubleday Dell Publishing Group, Inc. Its trademark, consisting of the words "Bantam Books" and the portrayal of a rooster, is Registered in U.S. Patent and Trademark Office and in other countries. Marca Registrada. Bantam Books, 1540 Broadway, New York, New York 10036.

PRINTED IN THE UNITED STATES OF AMERICA

OPM   0 9 8 7 6 5 4 3

To Anita Anastasi

Chapter 1

"Cameron, wait!" Jessica Wakefield pleaded as she watched the mirrored elevator doors slide shut, separating her from the guy she loved. She was left standing alone in the ninth-floor hallway of the Mode building, her heart sinking. *What have I done?* she asked herself.

Silence surrounded her like a thick, suffocating cloud. Most of the employees who worked in the chic Los Angeles high-rise wouldn't be arriving for hours.

Jessica had come in early, eager to catch a few minutes alone with her boss, Quentin Berg, to discuss the results of the photo shoot they'd done the previous day. Quentin was a world-famous fashion photographer, and even though Jessica was only a high-school intern, he'd allowed her to model for a very important fashion layout.

Not that he had much choice, Jessica thought

smugly. She'd worked *hard* to get herself into that shoot.

Quentin had previously shot the layout the day before using Simone, a supermodel with a super-obnoxious personality, who also happened to be Quentin's former girlfriend. Part of Jessica's job—the *worst* part—was having to put up with Simone's temper tantrums and constant demands for French mineral water and raw vegetables.

Jessica had taken the internship at *Flair,* the hottest new fashion magazine owned by the Mode Corporation, with only one thought in mind—to launch her modeling career. So yesterday, after Simone had left for the day, Jessica had discreetly opened Quentin's camera, exposing the film. There hadn't been time to call in another model, so Jessica had gladly stepped in to take Simone's place.

Only a few minutes ago she'd been happy enough to touch the stars. Quentin had just told her that her photographs had received a thumbs-up from *Flair'*s editorial board. Then he'd kissed her . . . at the very instant Cameron had walked into the studio!

Jessica slumped against the cold marble wall next to the elevator and closed her eyes. Hot tears streamed down her cheeks. *Talk about rotten timing!* Jessica thought. Cameron Smith, who worked in the mail room, was one of the sweetest guys she'd ever met. He was also gorgeous—with curly brown hair, impressive muscles, and big brown eyes. Unfortunately *he* wasn't the world-famous photographer

2

who could help her launch her career at *Flair*.

Jessica opened her eyes and pressed her fists against the smooth fabric of her turquoise pants. *Why did that jerk Quentin have to kiss me anyway?* she fumed. Aside from being a talented photographer, Quentin was an egotistical creep. He probably thought any girl would be thrilled to kiss him.

Fresh tears streamed down Jessica's cheeks as she recalled the expression of hurt and anger on Cameron's face as he'd gotten into the elevator. His features had appeared as if they'd been cut from stone, and his brown eyes had been glassy and cold. His parting words rang her in her ears: *It's over, Jessica. No more chances.* The memory felt like a hot knife tearing through her heart.

Jessica pressed her fists against her eyes. *Why can't Cameron understand how important my career is?* she wondered bitterly.

Jessica knew most people—even some of her teachers at Sweet Valley High—assumed that she wasn't serious about her future, that all she cared about were boys, shopping, and cheerleading. They seemed to think that her identical twin, Elizabeth, had inherited all the genes for logical thinking, maturity, and hard work.

But they were wrong. Granted, Elizabeth was clearly the more serious-minded twin. Older by four minutes, she was hardworking and reliable. She got straight A's in school, kept her room impeccably neat, and always remembered to do her

3

chores around the house.

Elizabeth hoped to become a professional writer someday and spent most of her free time writing for the *Oracle,* Sweet Valley High's student newspaper. Her idea of "fun" was to curl up with a book, organize her closet, or hang out with her boring friends, Enid Rollins and Maria Slater.

A bright spot in her sister's life—in Jessica's opinion—was Elizabeth's recent breakup with Todd Wilkins, one of the dullest guys in Sweet Valley. He'd started modeling for Quentin and was now dating Simone, but that didn't change Jessica's opinion of him. OK, *yes,* Todd was handsome, Jessica had to admit that. But he was still as boring as dry toast. She only wished Elizabeth would hurry up and get over him.

The differences between Jessica and Elizabeth were enormous, despite their identical appearance. They both had clear blue-green eyes, silky blond hair, and slim, athletic figures. In the past Elizabeth had usually worn her hair in a ponytail or braid, while Jessica had preferred to leave hers loose. But now even that small distinction was gone. Both sisters had recently gotten their hair cut to shoulder length, angled longer in front for a more stylish, modern look.

Jessica believed in living life to the fullest. Wild colors and loud music suited her best. Each day was a great adventure and much too precious to waste worrying about schoolwork. As long as her grades were high enough to maintain her position as co-captain on the cheerleading squad, she was satisfied.

Compared to her sister, Jessica hardly fit the image of a serious, ambitious, and intelligent sixteen-year-old girl—but that's exactly what she was. She dreamed of becoming a glamorous celebrity someday, and she was just as determined as her twin to achieve success.

Jessica sniffed and stood in front of the elevator. Pushing back her hair from her damp face, she stared at her reflection in mirrored door panel. Her eyes were red and puffy from crying. *I'm a mess!* she thought.

Jessica dabbed her fingertips under her eyes, careful not to mess up her makeup. She'd carefully selected her outfit that morning—slim-fitting, turquoise satin pants with a matching tunic and a pair of funky seventies-style platform sandals. The look was designed to make her appear taller. Jessica realized her height of five feet, six inches, was the biggest obstacle to her career since successful fashion models were closer to six feet tall.

I'm going to make it anyway, Jessica vowed. *I'll do whatever it takes.* Her internship would end in a few days, and she wasn't about to leave without achieving a strong foothold in the business.

But a small voice in her head asked doubtfully, *Even if it means giving up love?* Jessica groaned to herself. She would just have to find a way to make it up to Cameron, to make him understand that

5

she wasn't interested in Quentin at all.

Jessica stiffened as she heard footsteps coming down the hall. She knew it was Quentin by the distinct sound of his designer boots. Forcing her attention back to the present, she put on a cheerful smile and turned to face her boss.

In his early twenties, Quentin Berg was tall, with broad shoulders, mysterious gray eyes, and shaggy, reddish blond hair. As usual he was wearing faded jeans, today topped with a black T-shirt and a pale khaki vest. Jessica considered him fairly good-looking in a rumpled artist sort of way. Too bad he was a totally conceited jerk.

"What was that all about?" Quentin asked, his light brown eyebrows raised in question.

Jessica swallowed hard. "It was nothing," she lied. "The mail-room guy was just upset because I forgot to put a return address on a package."

Quentin smirked. "What a loser."

Seeing the smug expression on Quentin's face, Jessica was tempted to tell him the truth—that kissing him was the biggest mistake of her life. Then she remembered the photo shoot . . . and the fact that he might use her for another layout. She felt torn. She didn't want to blow her chances with Quentin, but her heart ached over what had happened with Cameron.

"Guys like that don't understand how meaningless their jobs are," Quentin said, his voice dripping with disdain. "I could have him fired, but what's the use? Another loser would just come along and take his place."

Jessica nodded, pretending to agree. But inside she knew Cameron was anything but a loser. She vowed to herself that as soon as her career took off, she'd drop Quentin and concentrate on getting Cameron back into her life. But until that time Jessica was stuck with the number one creep of the fashion-photography field.

"So Quentin," Jessica began, hugging his arm as they walked back toward the studio, "when is my next shoot?"

Quentin chuckled. "I'll have to think about it."

"What's to think about?" Jessica asked, batting her eyelashes up at him.

"I'm not sure you're ready for a full-fledged modeling career," he told her. "The fashion world is rough, Jessica. Modeling is more than a job—it's a lifestyle. We're talking lots of hard work . . . *total* commitment, with cutthroat competition every step of the way."

They'd reached the studio and were standing in the doorway, facing each other. "I know all that," Jessica insisted. "Believe me, I'm not afraid of hard work, and I'm one hundred percent committed. I know I have what it takes to make it as a supermodel."

Quentin gave her a long, measuring look. "Maybe you do." Then he pushed open the studio door and went in.

"I *definitely* do," Jessica countered as she followed

him through the main area of the studio, a huge, cavernous room strewn with ladders, lighting fixtures, small tables, and various props. "As a matter of fact, I think I'd be great in the swimsuit layout we're shooting tomorrow," she declared, even though she knew Simone had already been lined up for the job.

Quentin stopped at the door of his private office, one of the smaller rooms off the main area, and turned to Jessica. "You're certainly ambitious," he said, chuckling.

You have no idea how *ambitious,* Jessica thought wryly. She wasn't afraid to go after what she wanted. By taking advantage of every opportunity that came along, Jessica created her own good luck. She was determined to move in on Simone's position as a top supermodel—no matter what it took. *I'll even suck up to a total jerk if I have to!* Jessica thought.

Jessica stepped closer and gently placed her hand on Quentin's elbow. "I'm a lot easier to work with than . . . *some* models. More fun too," she added suggestively, trailing her fingers up his arm.

Quentin stared at her hand, then at her. "You're something else," he said wryly.

"How sweet of you to notice." Jessica draped her arms over his shoulders and flashed him a saucy grin.

Quentin leaned back, as if to put distance between them, but at the same time brought his hands up to frame the sides of her face. "What's going on here, Jessica? A few minutes ago I got the distinct impression you weren't interested in this sort of . . . extracurricular activity."

Jessica shrugged. "You caught me off guard, that's all."

"I see," he whispered, moving in for a slow, smooth kiss. Jessica closed her eyes, willing herself to respond as much as she could—or at least not to recoil from him.

When the kiss finally ended, Jessica exhaled with relief. "I should start getting the sets ready," she offered, looking for an excuse to avoid another kiss.

Quentin winked, obviously unaware of how she really felt about him. "If you're going to be a fashion model, we're going to have to work on your image . . . get you seen in the right places, with the right people." He paused. "I'm going to take you to the Edge tonight. That place is always good for a photo op."

A flash of excitement shot through her. The Edge was a very exclusive hot new techno club in downtown L.A.

"I'll pick you up at nine," Quentin said. "Be ready." Abruptly dropping the subject, he glanced at his watch and let out a low whistle. "Time's flying, babe," he said, snapping his fingers. "I'll be in the darkroom for a few hours. If Gordon Lewis calls, put him through. Otherwise take messages. There's a list of supplies we need on my desk. . . ."

Lost in her thoughts, Jessica nodded absently as Quentin barked out a few more orders. Excitement surged through her like electricity. *A photo op with a world-famous fashion photographer and my very own layout . . . I'm about to become a bona fide su-permodel!* she mentally cheered.

Sitting at her desk in her bedroom, Elizabeth pushed up the sleeves of her pale blue sweater as she reread the last few sentences on her computer screen. *This plan just might work!* she thought, pleased with what she'd written. Her internship at *Flair* had turned out to be a disaster, but she was ready to fight back. At lunch the previous day she and her friend Reggie Andrews, an assistant fashion editor at *Flair,* had come up with an idea to help Elizabeth get revenge for the terrible way she'd been treated during her internship.

Elizabeth hit the command to print the document, then stretched her arms high over her head. Her neck, shoulders, and back felt painfully stiff. She glanced at her wristwatch and was surprised to discover that it was nearly four-thirty in the afternoon. She'd been sitting at her desk since early that morning, totally absorbed in her writing.

Elizabeth got up and began pacing across her room. As part of a new career-education program, Sweet Valley High students had been given the opportunity to work as interns during the school's two-week miniterm. Elizabeth had been thrilled to land a position in the editorial department of *Flair.*

From the start she had given her all to her work, putting in extra hours and sacrificing her personal life when necessary. Although many of her assignments had been dull, routine chores such as filing and opening the mail—"scum work," her boss had called it—Elizabeth had also been allowed to do some higher-level tasks. She'd proofread articles, drafted a letter to a writer, and researched various topics. She'd felt driven to prove herself capable to her boss, Leona Peirson, whom she'd idolized.

Leona had appeared to be exactly the kind of woman Elizabeth hoped to become someday—bright, ambitious, energetic, and assertive. Her respect had meant everything to Elizabeth. When Leona had implied that her look could use some improvement, Elizabeth had dipped into her savings for a fashion makeover.

Besides all that, Leona had often encouraged her to share her thoughts and ideas for the magazine. Elizabeth had been determined to come up with at least one brilliant idea during her internship, something that would really impress her boss.

She had put together a proposal for a new column to be written exclusively by *Flair* readers. But Leona had treated Elizabeth's hard work as if it were nothing more than a toddler's scribbled crayon drawing.

And then, to top it all off, Elizabeth had been devastated to discover that Leona was planning to propose the new column to the publisher, Gordon Lewis, and *Flair*'s editorial board as her own idea!

I wish I'd listened to Reggie sooner, Elizabeth reflected. Her friend had tried to warn her about Leona's true nature—*nasty.*

Elizabeth stopped pacing and sat down on her bed, drawing her knees up to her chin. Leona was a cold-blooded snake. But even if Elizabeth did manage to get back at her—then what? *My life still won't be perfect . . . or even as good as it used to be,* she realized dejectedly. She pressed her forehead against the soft fabric of her faded blue jeans. She knew she couldn't blame all her problems on Leona Peirson.

Elizabeth's own self-centered ambition had caused her to sacrifice her relationship with her two best friends, Enid Rollins and Maria Slater. Her boyfriend, Todd, had started getting resentful because she didn't have any time to see him. And he'd walked out of her life after he'd been "discovered" by Quentin Berg. Now he was working as a fashion model—and dating one. Elizabeth groaned as she remembered the time when she'd walked in on Todd kissing Simone in the photography studio at the Mode building. The memory sent a sharp pain right into the pit of her stomach.

Elizabeth lifted her head and pushed her hair back from her face. She needed her friends more than ever. Although Reggie would certainly be a sympathetic listener, Elizabeth didn't think she'd understand. Reggie was much older—in her twenties. And she didn't know Todd. Elizabeth longed to share her sorrow with Maria and Enid, her best friends in the world. She knew that having them around would make everything seem . . . less horrible.

I've been such a jerk, she told herself, her heart sinking as she remembered how badly she'd treated them. Elizabeth now realized that some things were more important than getting ahead in the business world. She wondered if they'd ever forgive her.

"I'm going to find out right now," she resolved, reaching for the telephone next to her bed. Just as she was trying to figure out what she would say to them, she heard a soft knock on the door.

Assuming it was her mother or father, Elizabeth softly answered, "Come in." The door opened, and Elizabeth's jaw dropped.

Enid and Maria were standing in the doorway, each holding a small paper bag. Elizabeth stared at them, speechless . . . and incredibly happy.

Dressed in a calf-length burgundy skirt, matching vest, and deep blue blouse, Enid had obviously come straight from her job at the Morgan Literary Agency, where she was doing her internship.

Maria was spending the miniterm working backstage at the Bridgewater Theatre in downtown Sweet Valley. Although she'd "retired" from her successful career as a child actor when she was twelve, she still had the look of a star, with smooth ebony skin, large brown eyes, and a tall, elegant build. Maria's outfit—wide-leg jeans and a pale yellow, hippie-era smock top—reflected her eclectic, slightly offbeat style.

"We come in peace," Enid said.

13

"And frozen yogurt," Maria added, waving her bag.

Elizabeth swallowed hard, feeling a lump in her throat. "Can you guys ever forgive me for being such a jerk?"

Enid and Maria looked at each other and shrugged. "Of course," Enid said. "That's what friends are for, right?"

Maria chuckled. "OK, now that we've settled that, let's get to the serious stuff. We've got some important decisions to make, girls."

"Like what?" Elizabeth asked.

"Like what flavor we should start with," Maria replied. "Pineapple coconut or fudge ripple?"

Elizabeth laughed. "Pineapple coconut first, fudge ripple for dessert. You guys are the best," she added. She ran downstairs to the kitchen for bowls and spoons, then joined her friends for a frozen yogurt picnic on her bedroom floor.

Elizabeth was helping herself to a generous scoop when she noticed Maria and Enid exchange concerned looks. "What's the matter?" she asked them warily.

"Liz, we heard that Todd moved out of his house Tuesday night," Enid told her. "He's staying at Ken Matthews's."

Elizabeth felt a sharp ache squeeze her heart. Although she was terribly angry at Todd for cheating on her with Simone, the news saddened her. "That's too bad," she replied softly.

"Time for dessert," Maria announced as she

opened the carton of fudge ripple frozen yogurt. "How's everything at *Flair,* by the way? It's strange not to hear you rattling on about your internship," she teased.

Elizabeth groaned. "Please don't remind me how stupid I've been!" Enid and Maria stared at her with matching looks of astonishment.

"What happened?" Maria asked.

"I found out that it was all a big lie, that's what," Elizabeth replied. "I was completely wrong about Leona, about everything. . . ." She took a deep breath and told them all about her column proposal and Leona's condescending response. "When I was at Leona's condo on Monday, I found a tape recorder with a letter she'd dictated for herself, proposing *my* idea and passing it off as her own." Elizabeth remembered how angry she'd been at that moment, when she'd realized how Leona had betrayed her. "She'd actually inserted a note to remind herself not to let me see the letter!"

"That's terrible!" Enid cried.

Maria nodded. "But what were you doing at her condo?"

Elizabeth rolled her eyes. "Leona broke her leg skiing in Tahoe last weekend. She asked me to do her personal errands, water her plants, feed her cats, and cover for her at work because she doesn't want anyone to know she went skiing."

"So what are you going to do?" Maria asked.

Elizabeth flashed a mischievous grin and told

them about the plan she and Reggie had devised. "We're going to present the proposal ourselves," she explained. "Reggie is going to help me set up a meeting with Gordon Lewis, the hotshot new publisher of *Flair* magazine. If everything goes according to plan, my proposal will go to the board before Leona gets back."

Maria covered her mouth and pretended to gasp as though she were shocked at Elizabeth's scheming, and then she smiled. "That's brilliant!"

"I sure wish I could be a fly on the wall when you meet with Gordon Lewis," Enid said.

Why not? Elizabeth wondered as a marvelous idea popped into her mind. Smiling, she asked, "How would you guys like to get into the fashion industry?"

Chapter 2

Todd could barely keep his eyes open as he rode
along the Santa Monica Freeway with Howie
Kurtz, the real estate agent he'd called that morning. He was desperate to find an apartment after
spending two sleepless nights on the lumpy couch
in Ken Matthews's room.

"So . . . you're modeling for *Flair* magazine?"
Howie inquired.

Todd nodded, then covered his mouth to sti-
fle a yawn.

"How soon do you need an apartment?"
Howie asked.

"Immediately," Todd answered. He slumped
down into the seat and crossed his arms. He couldn't
believe how messed up his life had gotten in such a
short time. Elizabeth had been so caught up in her
internship, she'd forgotten about what was really

important—like making time for them to be together. One evening, when he'd gone to pick her up at *Flair,* she'd insisted he go wait for her in the photography studio where Jessica was working.

Todd had known Elizabeth was just trying to get him out of her hair because she had work to do, but he'd gone to the studio anyway. That was the event that had changed his life. He'd met Simone that day and had stepped into a modeling career.

Todd inhaled deeply and let his breath out slowly. Simone had captured his attention immediately. Tall, slim, with gorgeous ice blue eyes and incredibly long legs, she was one of the best-looking girls he'd ever seen—especially dressed as she had been, in a tiny white bikini.

Then Quentin Berg had asked him to pose for a few test shots with Simone. Although Todd had felt embarrassed and self-conscious at first, he had gradually relaxed enough to enjoy the experience. Quentin had invited him to come back and model for an actual fashion layout. Todd had happily quit his boring internship at Varitronics, his father's company, and began hanging out with Simone every night at the best hot spots in L.A.

Todd rubbed his hand over his mouth and stared out the window, bleary-eyed. He missed Elizabeth more than he could stand. He had gone to her office at *Flair* last Friday to try to apologize. Not only had she refused to see him, she'd humiliated him by announcing it over the intercom.

Todd had been sitting in the crowded waiting area, holding a bunch of red roses, when Elizabeth's voice had come blaring out of the phone speaker on the receptionist's desk: *Please inform Mr. Wilkins that I never want to see him again.* Todd cringed inwardly, waves of embarrassment crashing over him all over again at the memory.

"I'm going to take you to Manhattan Beach first," Howie was saying. "I have several listings over there that I think you'll like."

"Sounds great," Todd murmured. He closed his eyes and couldn't help nodding off.

He awoke a short time later, just as Howie was pulling up to a beautiful condominium complex. "Sorry I fell asleep." Todd yawned as he sat up straighter and rubbed his eyes.

"No problem," Howie replied breezily.

Todd gazed out the window, impressed by the manicured lawns and the expensive, late model cars in the parking lot. "Wow, this is great!" he exclaimed, suddenly feeling energized.

"This place has everything you requested," Howie said as he led Todd to a door on the east side of the building. "Pool, air-conditioning, sauna, whirlpool bath, microwave . . . I think you'll like it." He stepped back and let Todd enter first.

I'll say! Todd thought excitedly as he walked in. The apartment was huge, with a brick fireplace and a walk-out patio in back. Todd could already picture the parties he'd have. They could set up a barbecue grill on the patio . . . then head over to the pool for a late night swim. . . . *And no curfews,* he reminded himself.

"There's only one bedroom," Howie explained. "But a larger unit will be opening up at the end of the month."

"This is perfect," Todd said. "I'll take it."

"Great." Howie shook his hand. "The rent isn't too bad for Manhattan Beach." He named a price, then added the amount required for a security deposit.

Todd blanched. One month's rent would clean out his entire savings account. "There's no way I can afford that much," he admitted.

Howie looked at him with a bemused expression. "I figured that as a model working for *Flair* . . . "

"I'm just starting out my career. I've only been at it for a week," Todd explained, feeling rather foolish all of a sudden.

Howie's eyebrows drew together, as if he were deep in thought. "How much *can* you afford?" he asked.

Todd shrugged. "A few hundred a month, I guess."

Howie grimaced. "Come on, let's go," he said, heading for the door. "We're in the wrong neighborhood. With a few hundred dollars a month, you can't rent a toolshed around here."

Crestfallen, Todd followed. It seemed his modeling money wouldn't go as far as he'd thought. *I wonder if it's too soon to ask Quentin for a raise.*

❖   ❖   ❖

Jessica felt her heart pulsing excitedly with the beat of the techno music blaring through the speakers when she and Quentin arrived at the Edge that evening. *This is fantastic,* she thought, her eyes wide as she gazed around the club. The tables were stark white, the floors shiny black, and a shimmering disco ball hung over the dance floor. A flashing red neon light surrounded the walls, casting a dazzling glow on the ultramodern decor. The club was packed with a hip L.A. crowd, and the party atmosphere seemed to crackle with electricity.

Jessica felt totally alive and excited. Her ice blue silk dress glimmered in the neon lights. She'd gone home from work earlier than usual that afternoon to give herself extra time to get ready. And although Quentin hadn't said much about her appearance after he'd picked her up that evening, Jessica felt extremely pleased with herself.

Quentin looked great too. He'd traded his everyday rumpled-artist clothing for a black retro dress jacket, a white button-down shirt, and black jeans. Jessica noticed lots of girls eyeing him openly and flashing him flirty smiles.

"Let's get closer to the dance floor," Quentin told Jessica. "Okay!" she readily agreed. With her hand loosely on her hip, she strutted after him toward the dance floor. But before they'd reached it, Quentin stopped abruptly and led Jessica away to a nearby table.

"Why do we have to sit?" she asked, disappointed.

Quentin turned his chair so that he was facing the dance floor. "Look around, Jessica," he replied. "We're here to be seen . . . and this happens to be the best spot in the whole place."

Jessica nodded mutely and took the chair next to his. Although she would've preferred to dance, she figured she should take his advice seriously. After all, the only reason she was out with Quentin was because he could help her career.

"This is the driving force of the fashion industry, Jessica," Quentin declared. "The L.A. scene, where celebrities, models, and fashion designers come together to make it happen."

Jessica nodded again, then sat up straighter as she noticed supermodel Tina Baker approaching the table. The striking brunette moved with an easy grace, her short black beaded dress and heavy silver jewelry shimmering in the neon lights. Jessica had long admired her and had even met her briefly some time ago, the day her best friend Lila's parents had remarried.

Tina enveloped Quentin in a hug, then turned to Jessica with an open, friendly expression. "Didn't we meet at the Fowler wedding in Sweet Valley?"

"That's right," Jessica responded, flattered that the famous model had remembered her.

"Would you like to join us?" Quentin ask Tina.

"Just for a minute." Tina sat down next to Jessica, chuckling. "I have friends waiting for me across the room, but first I have to find out what a nice girl like you is doing here with this character," she said jokingly.

Jessica giggled. "I'm working as an intern at *Flair*, as Quentin's assistant."

"You poor kid," Tina responded with mock horror, then smiled. "An internship at *Flair* sounds interesting. Are you interested in a career in photography?"

"Modeling," Jessica replied immediately.

Tina Baker nodded thoughtfully, narrowing her eyes as she gazed at Jessica with a measuring look. "I can see it. You have great eyes."

Jessica grinned broadly. "Thanks."

They talked for a few more minutes, then Tina announced she had to go meet her friends. "It was great seeing you again, Jessica. Lots of luck with your internship and modeling." She blew a kiss at Quentin and walked away.

"She's really nice," Jessica marveled, feeling incredibly pleased.

"Don't tell me you fell for her act." Quentin snickered, shaking his head. "Poor Jessica. You'll have to get used to people kissing up to you just to get to me. It'll happen all the time."

Jessica rolled her eyes, amazed at Quentin's arrogance. *He really is a jerk!* she thought. But as tempted as she was to tell him off, she held back. She still needed Quentin's help to establish herself as a model.

Quentin moved closer to her. "Look. Here

comes André Marceau of Marceau designs. Smile and wave, Jessica."

Jessica automatically obeyed, following his gaze to a tall, skinny man with waist-length gray hair. The man glanced over at her and Quentin and returned their greetings with a slight flick of his wrist as he walked by.

"André and I go way back," Quentin told Jessica. "I remember a layout I did for him last year. We were shooting in Chile, right on the coast. Suddenly, halfway through the day, the clouds came rolling in off the ocean.

"I slowed down the shutter speed and switched to black-and-white film." He flashed Jessica a sideways grin. "Everyone thought I was nuts, but those shots turned out incredible."

"That's great," Jessica responded politely.

"Believe me, 'great' is an understatement," Quentin replied. "It's no surprise that I won the VH1 award for best fashion photographer. There's no one else out there in my class."

Jessica sighed wearily and lowered her eyes. *I'm happy being here,* she silently told herself as she studied her silver-lacquered fingernails. *Even if Quentin is a totally self-centered, arrogant creep.*

Jessica noticed a red-haired guy wearing a forest green jacket standing over to her right, talking to the people at the next table. The conversation appeared to be lively and animated, though she couldn't hear a word of it over the loud music.

Jessica's eyes nearly popped out of her head as she recognized him. "Is that really . . . ?" she choked.

"Eddie Rook, the drummer from Nuclear Hearth," Quentin provided.

"Oh, my gosh . . . *Eddie Rook*," Jessica exclaimed, her sullen mood forgotten. "I *love* Nuclear Hearth. I have all their CDs!"

A tall blond girl in a sleeveless black leather jumpsuit rushed over and gave the rock star a big kiss.

"That's Sophia Tolland," Quentin whispered in Jessica's ear. Jessica nodded. She remembered seeing the model's face on a recent cover of *Mirabella*.

Jessica studied the couple intently as they lingered at the other table. Eddie Rook was standing behind Sophia Tolland, his arms around her slender waist and his chin resting against her hair.

Jessica smiled softly. There seemed to be something special about celebrities, as if they were surrounded with a glittering, magical aura. She was thrilled to know that someday soon, she too would become part of the magic. *No matter what it takes, I'm going to make it as a supermodel . . . and world-famous celebrity,* she vowed. Even if it meant spending her evenings with a jerk like Quentin Berg.

Just then Sophia Tolland turned her head. "Quentin!" she shrieked, her eyes wide. Obviously thrilled, she led Eddie Rook over to Jessica and Quentin's table.

I can't believe this! Jessica thought, her stomach fluttering excitedly.

Quentin rose to his feet and exchanged double-cheek kisses with Sophia, then shook hands with Eddie Rook. Sophia held out her hand, showing off a huge solitaire diamond on her finger. "We're officially engaged," she announced.

"That's fantastic," Quentin replied enthusiastically. "I wish you two all the happiness in the world."

As the three stood chatting for a few minutes Jessica noticed Eddie and Sophia glancing down at her, as if wondering who she was. *Why doesn't Quentin introduce me?* she wondered hotly. Finally she stood up and looped her arm around Quentin's, hoping he'd get her unspoken message—*I'm here and I won't be ignored!*

Quentin flashed her a tight grin. "This is Jessica," he said, making it sound like an offhand remark.

Jessica stiffened at the vague, unflattering introduction. But she wasn't about to let Quentin's bad manners ruin the thrilling moment for her. "I'm so pleased to meet both of you," she said sincerely, trying not to sound like a dithering, starstruck fan.

"We're headed over to the bar," Eddie Rook told them. "Some of the guys from my band are throwing us an engagement party, and they've posted bodyguards to keep all the paparazzi away from our table. You two are welcome to join us."

Jessica's heart leaped to her throat. *A party with Nuclear Hearth!* she silently shrieked, fighting the urge to jump up and down. She imagined her friends' reactions. *Lila will be totally jealous.* . . .

Then she noticed Quentin was shaking his head. Jessica froze. *He can't possibly be turning down the invitation?* she thought, questioning his sanity.

"You *have* to come celebrate with us, Quentin," Sophia pleaded, batting her incredibly long eyelashes at him. "After all, the photographs you took of me for the Chanel layout are what made Eddie fall in love with me."

Her fiancé laughed. "I carried a crinkled-up magazine page in my pocket for months before I got the nerve to call her," he admitted. "So you really should come to the party."

Of course we should! Jessica's mind shouted. She held her breath, wishing she could plant the right words in Quentin's mouth.

"Thanks, but maybe some other time," Quentin finally replied, draping his arm around Jessica's shoulders. "I've got to stay here and baby-sit my underage date."

Jessica reeled back, blazing. Heat rose in her cheeks. *How dare Quentin humiliate me like that!* she raged silently, her fists clenched at her sides.

Eddie chuckled, and Sophia shot her a sympathetic smile.

Jessica grinned tightly and said nothing, though her face felt as if it might crack under the pressure. She would have loved to scream at Quentin at that very moment, but she didn't want to embarrass herself even more than he already had.

Jessica waited until Sophia and Eddie left, then turned to Quentin. "That was a terrible thing to say!" she spat out furiously.

Quentin patted her shoulder. "You seem to be in a bad mood tonight, Jessica."

"I am now!" Jessica snapped, shrugging off his arm.

"I don't see what you're so mad about," Quentin complained. "It hardly makes sense to join Eddie and Sophia at a paparazzi-free table since we're here to be seen. And besides, you *are* underage." He combed his fingers through his shaggy, reddish blond hair and flashed her a condescending smile. "I was only thinking of you, Jessica."

Jessica's temper flared hotter. "Thanks for the favor," she retorted bitingly.

As the evening dragged on, a sharp headache began to throb in the middle of her forehead. Jessica sat glumly, ignoring Quentin's cues to "smile and wave" at the celebrities who passed by. *I'm bored,* she realized, somewhat amazed. *I'm sitting in L.A.'s hottest new club, with a world-famous fashion photographer, meeting celebrities . . . and I'm totally bored!*

"Quentin, can't we get up and dance for a little while?" Jessica pleaded.

"No, the dance floor is too crowded," Quentin declared, shaking his head. "I don't want to give up this table just to get lost in that mob." He moved his chair closer to hers and pointed to someone across the room. "That's Jeffrey Lee, the model who's doing the Quest jeans commercials. I once worked with him on a fabulous layout for *GQ.* . . ."

Jessica slumped back in her chair as Quentin continued his boastful monologue. A moment later she caught herself counting the tubes of neon lights on the ceiling. *Some date,* she thought, reaching her limit of tolerance. She wasn't sure what would happen if she spent one more minute sitting with Quentin. *I'm either going to explode . . . or fall asleep!*

". . . then I took some shots with the mountain peaks in the background," Quentin was saying.

Jessica rose to her feet. "I think I need some fresh air," she announced.

Quentin looked up at her and nodded. "You do seem worn out," he remarked. "Maybe you should touch up your makeup a little too."

Jessica drew her lips in a tight smile, holding back the nasty response bubbling in her mind. She headed for the closest exit, her head high and her back straight. "What a creep," she mumbled under her breath.

Outside, the pounding techno music had faded to a muffled, rhythmic sensation beating through the walls of the club. She breathed the cool night air deeply and exhaled with a sigh of relief. She began walking. A soft breeze fluttered in Jessica's hair and along the bottom hem of her silk dress. The constant hum of city traffic surrounded her, punctuated with blaring car horns and the occasional roar of a motorcycle. Across the street a high-rise building spelled out its address with lighted windows against a dark background.

Jessica knew that being a successful model would require hard work and sacrifice. But she hadn't expected such torture. Aside from being a talented and famous photographer, Quentin Berg was a jerk and total bore.

Jessica walked around the corner toward the front entrance of the Edge. *If only I were here with Cameron tonight,* she thought sadly. She stopped and closed her eyes for an instant, picturing his gorgeous brown eyes, his soft lips. . . . *But what about your career?* a pesky voice in her head demanded.

"It's so unfair!" Jessica groaned to herself. She wished more than anything that Cameron and Quentin's positions were reversed—that Cameron was the famous photographer and Quentin was the nobody.

Jessica continued walking farther up the block, passing the line of people standing at the entrance of the Edge. She imagined the fun she might've been having at that moment with Cameron as her date. The evening would be absolutely fabulous. They would have danced together, no matter how crowded the dance floor was. When people stopped by their table, Cameron would introduce her respectfully. He'd want everyone to know how special she was, how deeply he cared for her.

Jessica smiled softly. With Cameron she still might have chosen to slip out of the nightclub—but certainly not by herself . . . and *not* because she had a headache.

Jessica's mind spun a delicious fantasy of herself and Cameron sitting in the Edge, their eyes locked in silent communication. Finally their longing desire for each other would become overpowering . . . and they'd have to steal a few private moments together. . . .

She reached the end of the block and turned around, slowing her pace to an easy stroll. She wasn't in any hurry to get back to Quentin.

Jessica noticed a white Porsche pulling up in front of a restaurant a few doors away. Despite her pensive mood, she couldn't help admiring the car's sleek, gleaming exterior.

When the Porsche stopped, a female valet in a fancy gray uniform, matching cap, and white gloves hopped out of the car. Her double-breasted jacket had gold braided ropes draped over the shoulders.

Jessica watched the entrance of the restaurant, hoping to catch a glimpse of the car's owner. *Someday I'll be able to drive a car like that,* she assured herself.

A guy with curly brown hair, wearing a dark tuxedo, came forward to take the keys from the valet. Jessica's heart skipped a beat. She stopped in her tracks and gaped at him. *Cameron?* she thought, stunned. She continued staring as the car pulled away from the curb and disappeared into the stream of heavy traffic.

But it couldn't have been him, Jessica reasoned. She didn't think Cameron could easily afford a meal at such a fancy restaurant, let alone a Porsche. But the guy had looked so much like him. . . .

A sharp ache pierced her heart. Tears pooled in

her eyes, blurring her vision and creating halos around all the lights. *I miss Cameron so much,* she realized sadly. Jessica decided it had been her own wishful thinking that had conjured up the vision of him in the Porsche. But even if he couldn't afford to drive a fancy car, Cameron was the guy she truly loved.

She recalled how angry he'd looked when he'd walked in on her and Quentin that morning. *What if I've lost Cameron forever?* she wondered, choking back a sob.

Jessica vowed to make it up to him as soon as possible. She'd go down to the mail room tomorrow and force him to listen to her explanation. *I'll bring him a nice lunch,* she planned.

Jessica dabbed her fingertips across her face, brushing away her tears. It was time to go back to Quentin and his dull version of partying.

The following morning Maria and Enid accompanied Elizabeth to the Mode building. Elizabeth had talked it over with Reggie the night before, and they'd both agreed that it would be useful to more have players involved in their plan.

Elizabeth felt a weird sensation as she stepped into Leona's office. The black lacquered desk was completely scattered with stacks of unopened mail, papers, magazines, and file folders. The computer was still on, the screen-saver program flashing white stars on a dark background. "I feel like she's going to walk in any minute," Elizabeth murmured as she lowered herself into Leona's leather chair.

Maria curled up in the chair on the other side of the desk. "Don't worry, Liz. Leona is miles away, with a broken leg."

Maria's outfit of a cashmere sweater and slim-fitting black moleskin pants, with silver hoops in her ears, was much too artsy and unique for the editorial department. But that didn't matter, because Maria was going to stay behind the scenes for most of their plan.

Enid walked over to one of the large windows on the far wall. "What a view!" she exclaimed. She was more conservatively dressed, in a black calf-length wool skirt with a cream-colored vest over a burgundy silk blouse.

"Will you get back here and pay attention!" Maria scolded jokingly. "We have business to conduct."

"I'll call Reggie," Elizabeth replied, picking up the phone.

Reggie joined them a moment later. "You've brought the reinforcements," she said, walking into the office with a welcoming smile. Elizabeth quickly made the introductions.

"OK, where do we start?" Reggie asked, tucking her hands into the pockets of her blue blazer. She was wearing a matching tailored skirt that was the same length as the jacket. "I have a meeting this morning, but it shouldn't take more than an hour."

"No problem," Elizabeth assured her. "We can handle setting up the meeting with Gordon Lewis."

33

Reggie's face brightened at the mention of *Flair*'s handsome, dynamic publisher. Elizabeth knew her friend had a secret crush on Gordon Lewis.

"Everyone know their lines?" Maria demanded after Reggie left for her meeting. Maria had been unanimously elected to be the director of this morning's caper because of her vast acting experience. As a child, she'd starred in a science fiction movie and several television commercials. And as she was rounding out her dramatic experience through her internship as a set designer at the Bridgewater Theatre company in Sweet Valley, everyone figured she was the perfect choice.

Maria pushed up the sleeves of her violet cashmere cardigan and began coaching them on the roles they would play. "Remember, Elizabeth, you're a *newly* hired assistant editor. Any questions you can't answer, go back to that point—you haven't been here long enough to know everything.

"And Enid," Maria continued. "You're supposed to be a secretary, not a jack-in-the-box. Tone down the enthusiasm. Put a hint of boredom into your voice."

Enid stuck out her tongue as soon as Maria turned her back.

Elizabeth snickered. "No matter how this turns out, I want you guys to know that I think you're the best friends in the whole world," she declared. "I don't know how to thank you."

"Next time *you* buy the frozen yogurt," Maria quipped. "Now let's get this show

34

rolling." She clapped twice. "Places, everyone!"

Enid and Elizabeth's "places" were the two chairs on either side of Leona's desk. Elizabeth opened the Mode phone directory and scrolled down to Gordon Lewis's extension.

"And . . . *action!*" Maria ordered. "Be sure to lower your voice and pronounce each word clearly, especially the endings. It'll counteract the squeaky babbling effect of being nervous."

"Thanks for the tip," Elizabeth replied dryly. "But what if my mind completely blanks out?"

Maria picked up the spiked message holder on Leona's desk and aimed the point threateningly. "I'll figure out a way to make you snap to attention," she said, laughing.

Elizabeth dialed the number to Gordon Lewis's office and tried to put the call on speaker phone so they could all listen.

Maria frowned. "Why can't we hear anything?"

"Oh, no!" Elizabeth whispered harshly. "I think I pushed the button for the intercom." She dialed again, grabbed the handset, and handed it to Enid. "I'm too nervous for high tech. Let's just do this the old-fashioned way."

A moment later Enid perked up. "Yes, hello. Ms. Wakefield would like to speak to Mr. Lewis," she said with authority.

Maria gave Enid a thumbs-up sign, then cued Elizabeth to take the phone. Elizabeth took a deep breath as she waited for Gordon Lewis to pick up

35

the call. The instant he came on the line, he asked, "Who is this?"

"Elizabeth Wakefield," she told him. "I'm a new colleague of Leona's at *Flair*."

"I wasn't aware they'd hired anyone new," he replied. "How long ago did you start?"

Elizabeth blanked out for a second, but Maria's encouraging expression snapped her out of it. "I was hired by . . . Mr. Jowerininerskily, last . . . um, month," Elizabeth answered.

"While I was on vacation?" Mr. Lewis asked sharply.

Elizabeth nodded, which was stupid, since Mr. Lewis couldn't see her. "That's right, during your vacation," she told him hastily.

"Figures they'd increase the editorial staff when I'm out of the country," he grumbled. But he seemed to accept Elizabeth's status. "What can I do for you, Ms. Wakefield?"

"I have an idea I'd like to discuss with you," she said, pleased with her confident tone. "I think it could bring in a lot of revenue for *Flair*. Actually I've been meaning to call you for some time, but I haven't because, well, you know how busy—"

Maria signaled with a finger dragged across her throat.

Elizabeth gulped, realizing she'd been babbling. She swallowed hard and forced herself to get back in control. "When would it be convenient for me stop in at your office and show you my idea?"

"Today's out." He paused, as if he were flipping through the entries in his appointment book. "And most of tomorrow too. I have a meeting across town in the morning. Why don't I stop in when I get back to the building, say around eleven?"

Elizabeth's jaw dropped. "Oh, you want to come *here*?"

"That would be easiest. But I'm afraid I don't even know where your office is," Mr. Lewis said. "I assume you're on the eleventh floor, right?"

"That's right," Elizabeth managed to choke out. "The eleventh floor. My office is . . . I'm in Leona's office—her *old* office. She's somewhere else." She caught a glimpse of Maria rolling her eyes.

"OK, I'll see you tomorrow around eleven, Ms. Wakefield," he said.

"I'm looking forward to it," Elizabeth replied. She hung up feeling scared but triumphant.

The girls exchanged high-five slaps. "We did it!" Enid cheered.

"You guys were great," Maria commented. "A few rough spots, but you handled them well."

Enid and Elizabeth grinned. "Hey, Liz. Who's Mr. Jowerin . . . whatever?" Enid asked.

Elizabeth laughed. "Beats me. I purposely made up an unpronounceable name that Mr. Gordon couldn't easily remember."

"That was smart," Maria said. "Now we have to get ready for act two—The Meeting."

Elizabeth nodded, her eyes wide. Suddenly the

37

impact of what she'd just done—and was *about* to do—hit her full force like a bucket of ice water splashed in her face. "I've got a meeting with the head of this company!" she shrieked. "Oh my gosh, I have to make this office look like it belongs to me." She jumped up and began frantically scooping up the papers on Leona's desk. "How am I going to pull this off?"

"You're just nervous, Elizabeth," Enid said reassuringly. "Which is perfectly normal under the circumstances."

Elizabeth uttered a hysterical-sounding laugh. "*Normal?* I must be totally *insane!* What if Gordon Lewis sees right through me?"

"Just relax and breathe deeply," Maria instructed.

"I can't relax. I have to *think!*" Elizabeth picked up Leona's brass cube paperweight and passed it nervously from hand to hand. "Let's see. . . . The presentation is ready to go, although it could use a bit of polishing. The materials are in Reggie's office. I hope Reggie doesn't have anything important scheduled tomorrow at eleven."

Elizabeth set the paperweight down and immediately picked it up again. "When are we going to practice for our meeting with Gordon Lewis?"

"I'll pick up Enid after I'm done at the theater and we'll come back here," Maria assured her, glancing at Enid with a questioning look.

"Sounds fine with me," Enid added.

"Thanks. I just hope I'm done in here by then,"

Elizabeth replied, gazing around the office. She spotted items that shouted "Leona Peirson works here!" everywhere she looked: an engraved plaque in the bookcase behind the desk . . . an old postcard pinned to the bulletin board, probably addressed to Leona . . . a personalized memo pad with Leona's name on every page. . . .

Elizabeth sighed wearily. "Finding and removing all traces of Leona is going to be an enormous task."

"We'll check it over when we come back," Maria offered.

As Elizabeth gathered up Leona's unopened mail a small, glossy envelope caught her eye. Curious, she ripped it open, then glanced at her friends. "It's OK for me to open Leona's mail," she remarked defensively. "She asked me to, so it's part of my job."

Maria and Enid both chuckled. "Don't worry, we won't turn you in for tampering with the U.S. mail," Maria said wryly.

"Even though it *is* a felony," Enid added.

Elizabeth pulled out a printed card and read it to herself. "It's an invitation to a party at the Bel Air hotel tonight. I've heard some of the editors talk about this. All the bigwigs in publishing are sure to be there—including Gordon Lewis." Elizabeth smiled brightly. "What luck!" she exclaimed.

"We're going?" Enid asked innocently.

Maria tucked her arm around Enid's elbow. "You have a lot to learn about subterfuge," she teased.

"I have to talk to Reggie about it," Elizabeth murmured, thinking aloud.

Elizabeth leaned forward and snapped her fingers. "Ms. Rollins, get Reggie Andrews on the phone and set up a lunch meeting next door at the Mission Café," she barked at Enid. "Then bring me a cup of herbal tea."

"Wow, Liz! You're more than good," Maria proclaimed. "You're *dangerous*."

All three girls laughed.

Chapter 3

I will make *Cameron listen to me,* Jessica vowed as she rode the elevator down to the lobby of the Mode building at lunchtime. She planned to surprise him with a gourmet meal, hoping to catch him off guard so he'd listen to her apology.

Jessica glanced down at the brown paper bag she held in her hands, in which she'd packed a loaf of fresh bread, assorted cheeses, strawberries, chilled sparkling cider, and chocolate cookies she'd baked herself. *How can he resist such a romantic lunch?* she thought, smiling.

When she reached the lobby, Jessica paused to check her appearance in the mirrored doors of the elevator. She'd worn a black leather miniskirt and deep purple satin jacket with black leather trim. The look was everything she'd wanted—elegant, fun, and sexy. *Perfect,* she silently congratulated herself. A wonderful feeling of anticipation tingled up her spine as she went off to search for Cameron.

Cameron usually spent his lunch hour outdoors, in the central courtyard of the Mode building, which he'd jokingly named "Chez Bench." Before stepping outside, Jessica hastily finger-combed her hair and took a deep, bracing breath.

Shading her eyes from the glaring sunlight, Jessica scanned the area. He wasn't there. *Maybe he couldn't get out for lunch today,* she reasoned, swallowing her disappointment. She hoped that if Cameron had to work during his lunch hour, he'd be extra grateful to her for bringing him such a marvelous lunch.

Jessica smiled brightly as she strolled into the mail room. Unlike the posh lobby and high-tech photography studio, the mail room was a shabby maze of cluttered storage nooks, sorting areas, and loading docks. A guy with long blond hair, wearing a faded flannel shirt, was stacking boxes in a corner. "Can I help you, miss?" he asked.

"I'm looking for Cameron," Jessica told him. "Do you know if he went out for lunch?"

The guy shrugged. "I'm the only one here right now. If Cameron is the guy who used to work here, he's gone. I took his place."

A thick, cold feeling sank into the pit of her stomach. "Gone?" she echoed.

The new mail clerk nodded. "He quit. Is there anything I can help you with?"

Jessica tossed the guy her bag of her food and ran out of the room. She'd suddenly lost her appetite.

Later that afternoon Elizabeth returned to Leona's condo with Enid and Maria. "This won't take long," Elizabeth said as she unlocked the front door. She wouldn't have come back at all if it weren't for the cats. It wasn't fair to let them starve just because their owner was a lying snake.

"This really is gorgeous," Maria remarked as she followed Elizabeth inside.

Elizabeth shrugged. Leona's condo was breathtakingly beautiful, with high cathedral ceilings and pale wood floors. The living room was a huge open space; the far wall was made entirely of windows, and the colors of a spectacular sunset flooded the room. Over to the left two black leather couches were arranged perpendicularly around a glass table. A blue art deco clock hung on the wall, and shell-pink Tiffany lamps added a softening touch to the stark decor. "Leona has good taste," Elizabeth stated blandly. "I have to give her that."

"I think your customers have arrived," Enid said as two Persian cats came rushing into the room. She bent down to pet one, then jerked back her hand. "Ouch, he bit me!"

"They must be *so* hungry," Elizabeth said, feeling a pang of guilt for having neglected them for two days. She hurried into the kitchen, with the two cats yowling at her feet.

"I know, it was terrible of me not to come sooner," Elizabeth apologized as she opened a can of cat food. She was about to scoop it into the two ceramic cat dishes on the floor when an impish idea popped into her head. "I think you guys deserve better."

Elizabeth went into the formal dining room and opened the black china closet. "I think Leona's cats should dine in style tonight," she announced cheerfully as she removed two elegant white dinner plates rimmed with gold.

In the kitchen Elizabeth piled a large heap of cat food on each plate. *"Bon appétit,"* she said, setting them on the floor.

Pleased with herself, she returned to the living room. Maria and Enid were sitting on the black leather couches, their stocking feet propped up on the glass table. Maria's cashmere cardigan was bunched up behind her head as a pillow, and the shirttails of Enid's burgundy blouse were sticking out of her black skirt. "I see you've made yourselves right at home," Elizabeth remarked, chuckling.

Her smile froze on her face as she noticed the small tape recorder on the side table, right where she'd left it Monday. "I want you both to hear this," she told her friends. She turned on the recorder and Leona Peirson's deep, brisk voice filled the room.

"Letter to Gordon Lewis," Leona was saying. "Note to myself. This letter is not to go through Elizabeth."

Enid gasped and Maria bolted upright, but neither uttered a word.

"Dear Gordon," the recording continued. "As you suggested, I would like to formally submit the idea we discussed on the phone. . . . I propose a column tentatively titled 'Free Style,' a one-page article written by a *Flair* reader with her ideas on fashion. . . . I would be happy to discuss my idea at the next editorial board meeting. . . ."

Elizabeth slumped down next to Enid on the couch. Even though she knew the contents of the letter and could probably recite most of it from memory, hearing it again left Elizabeth feeling as shocked as when she'd first discovered the recording.

"That woman is *vile!*" Maria declared after they finished listening to the recording.

Enid agreed. "She even used *your* title for the column!"

Elizabeth plunked her feet up on the couch and grinned. "Leona will soon get exactly what she deserves."

"That reminds me," Maria said, jumping to her feet. "We need to go over the fine points for your meeting with Gordon Lewis tomorrow." She began pacing around the room. "It's the small details that can make or break a convincing performance."

She turned to Enid. "Remember to address Elizabeth as Ms. Wakefield at all times," Maria instructed. "You'll have to serve coffee when Gordon arrives. I suggest you bring cups and saucers from home so you'll be sure to have them ready. Bring a tray too."

Enid gave her a stiff, military salute. "Yes, ma'am."

"And remember, Elizabeth, as a corporate

executive, you never 'use' anything—you *utilize* it," Maria continued. "Actually you should tack on an *ize* to as many words as you can. It'll make you sound more convincing."

"Got it," Elizabeth replied. "And now if you two will excuse me, I've got some houseplants to *waterize*."

"And I have to *telephonize* my mother and let her know I'm going to be home late," Enid said.

Maria shook her head, laughing. "You two are hopeless."

In the kitchen Elizabeth turned on the sink and filled the blue watering can she'd used the last time she'd been there. Glancing down at the cats, she giggled. They seemed to be thoroughly enjoying their elegant dining experience.

"Reggie seems really nice," Enid commented when Elizabeth returned to the living room. "But isn't it possible that she's just as ruthless as Leona?"

"No, Reggie isn't like that at all," Elizabeth insisted. "She's really a sweet person."

Maria snorted. "How could anyone working in the Mode empire be *sweet?* Look what working there did to *you* in just a few days."

Elizabeth flinched as if she'd been stung. "I suppose I deserved that."

"I was just teasing," Maria insisted.

"But getting back to Reggie," Enid interjected. "What if she's just another Leona in training? She might be trying to claw her own way up the corporate ladder."

"No way," Elizabeth replied. "Reggie's career is important to her, but it's not her whole life. She wants to get married someday and raise a family." Elizabeth reached up to water a hanging ivy plant. "Reggie's been in love with Gordon Lewis for ages. But she's never had the courage to speak to him."

"That's sort of cute," Enid said.

Maria nodded. "Yeah, it is. Maybe there's something we can do to help. At the very least we can push them together tonight," she suggested.

"We'll make her look absolutely irresistible," Elizabeth added, another great idea taking shape in her mind. "Not that Reggie isn't already beautiful. But we have to find something absolutely stunning for her to wear. And I know exactly where to look. . . ."

"I like the idea, but we still have to drive back to Sweet Valley and get ourselves dressed up for the party," Enid pointed out. "We don't have time for an emergency shopping trip to search for an *absolutely stunning* outfit for Reggie."

"Just leave it to me," Elizabeth said. "I'll call Reggie and tell her to come over right now."

"Oh, sure, and maybe we can hold a quick bake sale or a car wash to pay for her stunning outfit," Maria remarked sarcastically.

Elizabeth shook her head. "We're not going to *buy* anything, just . . . borrow. Leona has tons of stuff in her closets. We can all get ready for the party right here."

Enid and Maria looked at her with matching dumbfounded expressions.

"It'll be fine," Elizabeth assured them.

Maria turned to Enid. "I *told* you she was dangerous."

"Trust me," Elizabeth insisted. "Leona won't be back for days, maybe weeks. And by the time she does get back, a few extra wrinkles in her fancy outfits will be the least of her problems."

They went upstairs and searched through the huge walk-in closet in Leona's bedroom. "Let's concentrate on finding something for Reggie first," Maria suggested, "since she's the leading lady of tonight's performance."

Elizabeth flipped through a few outfits. "I just found it," she announced, pulling out a short black dress with a deep neckline and suede trim. She carried it on its hanger to the bed and laid it out for her friends to see. "It's a Lina Lapin design," Elizabeth explained.

Maria looked it over and nodded. "It's sensational. Gordon Lewis won't know what hit him!"

Enid inhaled deeply and sighed. "I feel like a fairy godmother."

"This is it," Todd announced as he and Ken pulled up in front of an old Victorian house in an older neighborhood near Hollywood.

Todd stepped out of his black BMW and gazed at his new home. He was surprised at how shabby the place appeared. The drab gray paint was cracked and chipped, the front porch sagged, a broken window on the second floor was pieced together with duct tape. Howie had shown Todd the apartment the night before, but it had been dark outside and the house hadn't seemed so . . . *ugly*.

"It's huge," Ken commented. The guys each grabbed an armload of boxes and duffel bags from the trunk of Todd's BMW.

"It's divided into apartments," Todd explained as he led the way to the front entrance. There was a gaping hole in one of the door panels. "I guess the super must be on vacation," he mumbled dryly. Inside, the hallway smelled like old cabbage and wet dogs. "What's it like to be going out with a big-time model?" Ken asked as they climbed the stairs to Todd's fourth-floor apartment.

"Simone is awesome," Todd answered automatically. "A few nights ago we went to the Edge, a techno club downtown. There was this crowd of like a hundred people at the door, trying to get inside. Simone and I went right up to the front of the line, and the bouncers waved us right in."

"Must be great." Ken sounded impressed.

"It's amazing," Todd agreed, forcing himself to sound more enthusiastic than he actually felt. "The real exclusive places have a list of the people they'll let inside, like rock stars, famous actors, billionaires, and"—he paused for effect—"top fashion models."

"What's it like inside those places?" Ken asked.

Todd shifted his duffel bag to his other hand. "Like the best party you've ever been to, times a thousand."

Ken chuckled. "That good, huh?"

"Out of this world," Todd said. "Great bands, beautiful girls everywhere you look . . ." He didn't add how much he missed Elizabeth, how empty his life felt without her.

At door of his apartment Todd reached into the front pocket of his jeans and took out his keys. "It's not too big, but it's all mine," he declared triumphantly as he unlocked the door.

Todd walked into his apartment, and his heart sank. Like the exterior of the house, the place looked a lot worse than it had the night before. The living-room carpet was a grungy, sickly orange color, worn thin in spots. The walls were stained with brown streaks, and a thick, dark spiderweb draped down from the ceiling.

"It'll look a lot better once I get my stuff in here," Todd said, trying to sound cheerful. "Maybe a little paint on these walls . . . it'll be great."

Ken leaned back against the living-room wall and folded his arms, his expression grave. "Make that *lots* of paint."

"Okay, lots of paint," Todd returned bitingly.

Suddenly Ken jumped forward, shaking his arms. "I felt *something*," he muttered. "Look, there it is!"

Following Ken's gaze, Todd saw a huge centipede dash up the wall and disappear into a crack in the woodwork. "Cool. I even get to trap my own dinner," he joked, gulping down his revulsion. Ken wandered over to the tiny kitchen off the living room. "Don't bother," he called a moment later.

"With what?" Todd asked.

"They've already left dinner for you."

Bemused, Todd went over to investigate. The kitchen was every bit as ugly as the living room, with cracked linoleum on the floor and ratty old curtains in the window above the sink. A cheap white plastic patio table and chairs were set up in the corner. The kitchen appliances were probably older than Todd.

Ken opened the refrigerator and a nasty, sour stench wafted into the room. "Old milk and shriveled-up pizza," he said.

"Sounds delicious," Todd replied sarcastically. "You can close the refrigerator now."

Todd peered into the oven. It appeared to be standard quality, with a broiler and two racks. Everything was coated with a thick layer of dark grease, but Todd figured he could take care of that with some detergent and steel wool. *This is really mine*, he realized, a tiny flicker of interest springing to life inside him.

Ken ambled over to the table and sat down in one of the plastic chairs. "So Todd, now that you're busy with Simone, would you mind if I asked Elizabeth out?"

Todd felt as if he'd been punched in the stomach. Then a sudden, bone-chilling anger gripped his heart. He slammed the oven door shut and slowly turned around. "Ken . . . ," he began, his

51

voice smooth and steady as a steel knife, "if you go anywhere near Elizabeth, I'll break your nose."

Ken raised his hands and laughed. "I was just kidding. One Wakefield twin was enough for me." He and Jessica had dated steadily for some time until she'd cheated on him with a guy from a rival school. Todd knew that Ken wasn't completely over the ordeal.

"Really, I was kidding," Ken assured him.

"You'd better be," Todd warned. But he remembered that Ken and Elizabeth had had a brief, secret fling when Todd had temporarily moved to Vermont. What if she and Ken decided to pick up where they'd left off?

Todd opened and closed kitchen cupboards, absently noting their contents. But all he was aware of at that moment was his stomach twisting into knots. Elizabeth was a great girl—and now she was free. Even though Ken was only kidding, Todd knew it wouldn't be long before some guy did ask her out. *It's my own fault,* Todd thought, mentally kicking himself for losing her.

Suddenly a burst of angry shouting erupted in the apartment next to Todd's. Something crashed against the wall, the force of the impact strong enough to shake Todd's stove and refrigerator. A stream of curses, male and female, followed the crash. "Live entertainment," Ken quipped.

"Great," Todd uttered dryly. "Since I don't have a TV yet . . . or a phone."

Ken pushed his hands deep into the pockets of his denim jacket and glared at him. "Todd, this place is a dump."

"It's not *that* bad," Todd argued weakly. "With a little fixing up, it might be OK."

Ken's lips twisted in a sarcastic grin. "Yeah, *right*. And with a little intense psychotherapy your neighbors might be OK." He shook his head. "You don't have to live here. You can stay at my place until you find something better," Ken suggested.

Todd was tempted. Just thinking of having to clean out the smelly refrigerator made him sick. But he remembered the looks on his parents' faces when he'd stormed out of the house Tuesday night, when he'd finally had it with their attempts to control him. *They think this is all a childish prank,* he told himself. *They're waiting for me to fall flat on my face and come running back to Sweet Valley.*

Todd refused to let that happen. Even if his parents had zero confidence in his ability to make it on his own, Todd believed in himself. And he was determined to prove it to his parents.

Todd sat down across from his friend and flattened his palms against the table. "I appreciate your offer, Ken, but finding a better place isn't the problem. Right now I can't afford a fancy apartment . . . or even a decent one," he admitted. "But soon I'll be getting more modeling jobs and making big money."

"I can't believe you're serious about living in this dump," Ken argued.

Todd looked him straight in the eye. "I'm going to live here," he replied. "And I'm *very* serious."

"Oh, wow!" Elizabeth breathed, her eyes wide as she walked into the party at the Bel Air hotel with her friends that evening. The air seemed to crackle with energy. The room was filled with lavishly dressed people talking in small groups and sipping champagne. Elizabeth recognized several famous faces from photographs in magazines and on book jackets.

Waiters wearing red tuxedo jackets and balancing trays of champagne glasses over their heads wove through the crowd. A buffet had been set up along the far wall, with a huge, spiral-shaped ice sculpture in the center of the table. On the other side of the room a string quartet was performing on a raised dais, the strains of classical music just loud enough to be heard above the muted buzzing sound of the many conversations among the guests.

"Wow, *everyone's* here!" Reggie whispered.

"Shouldn't we mingle?" Enid asked.

Elizabeth shook her head, gripped with panic. *I'm not ready for this,* she thought. Even in a glamorous opal chiffon dress—a Pierre Jové original—and silver high-heeled sandals, she felt as if the words *sixteen-year-old impostor* were tattooed on her forehead. "What if they throw us out?" she murmured.

Maria squeezed her hand. "Why would they? Are you planning to start a food fight?"

Enid and Reggie chuckled, but Elizabeth just

stared straight ahead, too nervous to appreciate her friend's attempt at humor. "What if everyone figures out that we're teenagers crashing the party?"

"Come on, Elizabeth," Maria gently chided. "We look just as grown-up and snazzy as everyone else here."

Elizabeth exhaled slowly. Maria was right. She had used her stage makeup skills to make herself, Elizabeth, and Enid look older. And they all *did* look fabulous—thanks to the outfits they'd "borrowed" from Leona's closet. The black Lina Lapin dress was a perfect fit for Reggie. It showed off her slim figure and long legs to perfection, as if the designer had created it with her in mind. Leona's clunky silver earrings and chain necklace added the finishing touches.

Enid looked incredible in a shimmering lime green velvet gown, with silver mesh earrings and matching bracelet. Maria had chosen a long, floral print silk skirt and a tailored black leather sleeveless jacket with gold buttons. A matching leather bag hung over her shoulder.

"We all look wonderful," Reggie said.

"Now, are we going to get this show on the road, or what?" Maria asked impatiently.

Elizabeth took a deep breath and let it out slowly. They'd come to this party to set the stage for her meeting with Gordon Lewis the following day—and to help get him and Reggie together. Elizabeth wasn't about to give up, no matter how many butterflies fluttered in her stomach. "It's now or never, I guess," she said, steeling her courage.

Maria pushed the strap of the leather bag farther up her shoulder. "Reggie and I will look around for Gordon. Elizabeth and Enid, you two should probably find a corner and hide for a while."

"Gee, thanks," Enid grumbled.

Maria pursed her lips. "We don't want Gordon to see you or Elizabeth until the meeting tomorrow. But I promise we'll come tell you as soon as we've spotted him."

Elizabeth nervously rubbed a fold of her gray chiffon dress between her fingers. "Where should we wait?" she asked.

"There aren't many people around the banquet table," Maria observed. "Let's meet there."

Reggie pressed her bottom lip between her teeth and rolled her eyes. "I still can't believe I'm doing this," she whispered as she and Maria turned to go.

Elizabeth and Enid exchanged furtive looks and headed toward the banquet table. Unaccustomed to wearing such flimsy, high-heeled shoes, Elizabeth took small, slow steps to avoid losing her balance. *Please, don't let me fall on my face*, she silently prayed as she eased her way through the crowd.

When she finally reached the buffet, Elizabeth gripped the edge of the linen-covered table and breathed a sigh of relief. Enid wobbled up next to her. "They should put a warning label on these ridiculous shoes," Elizabeth grumbled.

Enid took two plates from a stack next to the

ice sculpture and handed one to Elizabeth. "As long as we're here, we might as well enjoy ourselves," Enid suggested. She helped herself to some black caviar from a crystal bowl on ice.

Elizabeth selected a bite-size pastry shell filled with pâté and truffles, then added some shrimp cocktail and a small serving of spinach salad to her plate. Just as she popped the flaky pâté tart into her mouth, a woman with short-cropped dark hair, wearing a glittery white beaded dress, came up to her. "Excuse me, didn't we meet in Milan last spring?" she asked Elizabeth.

Startled, Elizabeth shook her head.

"I'm positive we did," the woman insisted. "You're with *Vogue,* right?"

"You must have me mixed up with someone else," Elizabeth replied. "I'm not . . ." Suddenly she felt some crumbs brushing against her lips, falling to her chin, and she realized she was talking with her mouth full. Totally embarrassed, Elizabeth clamped her teeth together and pressed her fingers over her lips. Her face felt as though it were on fire.

Enid stepped in to help. "Liz decided not to go to Milan this year," she told the woman in a casual tone. "But she went lots of other places. Because she's a very important fashion editor . . . but not at *Vogue.*"

The woman gave them a strange look and walked away, shaking her head.

"That went well," Enid muttered sarcastically.

Elizabeth swallowed, then drew in a shaky

breath. Just then she saw Reggie and Maria hurrying toward them.

"He's in the bar," Reggie announced, choking out the words.

Maria glared at Elizabeth's plate with a look of horror. "Liz, please don't tell me you're eating that salad."

Elizabeth frowned, bemused. "I haven't yet. What's wrong with it?"

Maria grabbed the plate away from her. "What's *wrong* is that we don't have any dental floss with us. Once you speak to someone with spinach stuck in your teeth, you'll lose their respect *forever*."

Enid giggled. "That's quite profound, Maria." But Elizabeth mentally swore an oath never to eat in public again.

Maria and Reggie led the way to a circular alcove on the other side of the private banquet room. Standing near the entrance, Elizabeth peered inside. A polished oak bar dominated the area. Black tables were arranged along the perimeter. Elizabeth spotted Gordon Lewis sitting alone at the far end of the bar. Tall, with bright blue eyes, brown hair, and chiseled features, he was one of the handsomest men she had ever seen. She pointed him out for Enid.

Enid's eyes widened. "He's *gorgeous!*" she exclaimed.

"*I* think so," Reggie added. She drew in a

shaky breath. "What if I go up to him and he brushes me off?"

"Have you seen yourself in a mirror lately?" Maria questioned. "In *that* dress you should worry that he might fall off his seat and hurt himself."

Reggie uttered a shaky laugh. "I'm so nervous."

"Use your feelings," Maria advised her. "Acting is about honesty."

Enid wrinkled her nose. "What are you talking about? Acting is about making believe."

Maria glared at her. "Excuse me, who's the director of this show?"

"Director?" Enid asked pointedly. "Or *dictator*?"

Maria shrugged. "They mean the same thing." She turned to Reggie. "Gordon is a bigwig in the company you work for. It's perfectly natural to feel a bit jittery. Let it be part of your act."

"What if I'm so nervous, my voice chokes up and I can't speak?" Reggie asked.

"Too bad we're not doing a musical," Enid interjected. "Then you could burst into song whenever you got too nervous."

The others groaned. "I can teach you some of the tunes from *Evita*," Maria joked. It was the musical she was working on at the Bridgewater Theatre company.

"Okay, this is it," Reggie declared softly. "Watch for my signal." With her shoulders back and her head held high, she glided over to the bar.

Holding her breath, Elizabeth waited to see if the encounter would go according to plan.

Chapter 4

Standing between Enid and Elizabeth, Maria watched Reggie glide over to Gordon Lewis, her arms gracefully at her sides and her chin raised just enough to project self-confidence. The stool next to his was vacant, and Maria wondered how Reggie would handle it.

Don't sit down immediately, Maria thought, wishing she could send telepathic stage directions to Reggie. *Make him think you might walk away any minute.*

Reggie rested her arm on the bar—and remained standing. "Yes!" Maria breathed, clenching her hand into a victorious fist. Gordon and Reggie began talking. "I wish I knew how to read lips," Enid whispered.

"Read their faces," Maria replied. "Gordon's blue eyes are flashing with enough electricity to light up three city blocks."

Enid giggled. "Handy guy to bring along on camping trips."

"They do seem to like each other," Elizabeth remarked.

"It's so *romantic*." Enid sighed. "They make such a beautiful couple."

A tall, stunning woman with chin-length blond hair walked into the room. Wearing a shimmering deep green beaded dress and diamond jewelry, she sparkled with countless dots of reflected light. "There's another one to invite on your next camping trip, Enid," Maria joked.

"I love her dress," Elizabeth murmured.

Suddenly the woman rushed over to Gordon Lewis and they exchanged a warm hug. Maria gasped. Enid and Elizabeth uttered strangled sounds of horror.

"Tell me this isn't happening," Enid whispered.

"Poor Reggie," Elizabeth said woefully. "This was supposed to be her big chance with Gordon."

"Do you think we should go in there and rescue her?" Enid suggested.

"She's not being held prisoner," Maria pointed out.

Suddenly Elizabeth turned her head sharply to the side and did a double take. Her gaze seemed to be focused on a brown-haired guy in a tuxedo who was walking out of the room. "Cameron?" Elizabeth blurted incredulously.

Nonplussed, Maria stared at her. "Cameron who?" she and Enid asked in unison.

Elizabeth shook her head. "Never mind. I just

caught a glimpse of someone who reminded me of the guy from the mail room at the Mode building," she explained. "Jessica has been seeing him. But it couldn't have been him."

"Not likely, if he works in the mail room," Enid replied.

Maria saw Reggie rubbing the side of her nose. "There's my signal," she said, reaching into her leather evening bag. She took out the compact cellular phone that they'd "borrowed" from Leona and dialed the number for the local hot line that played a continuous recording of weather information.

"Break a leg, Maria," Elizabeth said.

Maria chuckled. "I'm wearing a long silk skirt and five-inch-heel shoes, so I just might."

"If that happens, you can call Leona and commiserate together," Enid joked.

"Doesn't that sound like fun," Maria replied dryly over her shoulder. Strolling into the bar, she eased herself into character. She was playing the role of a freelance writer who'd worked often with Reggie and Elizabeth.

"Maria," Reggie called, her eyes projecting a look of delighted surprise.

Maria approached the bar, giving Gordon and the blond woman a brief smile before turning back to Reggie. "Reggie Andrews, you're *just* the person I wanted to see," Maria told her. "I have Elizabeth Wakefield on the phone. She's been trying to reach you all evening."

Reggie took the cellular phone from Maria and smiled apologetically at Gordon and the other woman. "Excuse me, but I really do have to take this call." She held the phone up to her ear. "Elizabeth, I thought you'd be here hours ago. . . . You're *where?* . . . That's incredible . . . and he's giving us an exclusive? . . . No, I promise I won't breathe a word of it. . . . *Really?* . . . His designs for the Paris show? . . ."

Pressing her bottom lip between her teeth, Maria closely observed Reggie's performance. *The monologue is bit rushed . . . but her facial expressions are superb,* she thought. She spotted Elizabeth and Enid standing outside the bar, watching anxiously. Maria secretly gave them a brief, hopeful smile.

Reggie ended her "call" and folded up the compact phone. "Thanks, Maria," she said, handing it back to her. "I'm glad Elizabeth was able to reach me."

"You're very welcome," Maria replied, slipping the phone back into her bag. "I know with Elizabeth it's always something vital."

Reggie introduced Maria to Gordon and to Geneva Clark. "Geneva is a painter and sculptor," Reggie said. "She just arrived a little while ago from a two-week trip to London."

Maria shook hands with them, then glanced at Reggie, trying to understand exactly what was going on with her. Reggie seemed to like Geneva Clark, and Maria was almost positive it wasn't an act.

"Elizabeth Wakefield. What a coincidence,"

Gordon commented after the introductions had been made. "I just spoke with her this morning."

Reggie smiled. "She's fabulous, isn't she? Everyone says Elizabeth is the hottest new voice in the fashion industry. And from working with her, I have to agree."

"I've never met her," Gordon said. "But I have a meeting with her tomorrow."

Geneva Clark reached over and daintily picked out a cashew from the crystal bowl on the bar. "I know an *Alice* Wakefield," she mentioned casually. "I wonder if they're related."

Maria blanched at the mention of Elizabeth's mother's name. "Distantly, maybe," she uttered in a strangled voice. *As in the distance between L.A. and Sweet Valley,* she added silently.

Geneva Clark pulled the nut bowl closer. "Gordon, you remember Alice Wakefield, the designer who decorated my loft last year? I'm having her redo the beach house."

"Vaguely," Gordon replied.

Maria nervously fingered the clasp of her leather bag. *That woman is going to ruin everything,* she worried.

Gordon turned to Reggie. "Elizabeth Wakefield wants to tell me about an idea she has for *Flair.* Do you know anything about it?"

"No, I don't," Reggie replied brightly. "I've been assisting her on several different projects—it could be any one of them. But I'll give you a tip,

Gordon. If Elizabeth Wakefield offers you an idea, you should grab it. Other magazines have been clamoring to recruit her away from *Flair* since the day she arrived."

"Interesting," Gordon replied, cupping his chin with his hand. "I'm looking forward to meeting her."

OK! Maria cheered silently. Elizabeth would finally get to present her idea for "Free Style" to someone who took her seriously.

"Thanks for your advice, Reggie," Gordon said. "Meeting you may be one of the best things that ever happened to me. For several reasons," he added in a low, sexy voice.

Maria glanced at Geneva Clark to see her reaction. To her surprise, the woman seemed totally oblivious. She was munching salted nuts with a perfectly contented look on her face.

Just then she stood up and smoothed her hands over her exquisite green dress. "I'm going to go check out the buffet," she announced. "After two weeks of that ghastly British cuisine I'm *starving*."

"That's a great idea," Maria blurted.

Geneva winked, then shot Gordon a teasing look. "I'd better get my fill now because I know there won't be anything good to eat in your apartment."

His apartment? Maria silently shrieked.

"You're right," Gordon said, chuckling as he rose to his feet. "I'll go with you." He invited Maria and Reggie to join them, but Reggie declined for them both.

65

The instant Gordon and Geneva left, Elizabeth and Enid came rushing over to the bar. Reggie slumped onto the barstool and burst out laughing.

"What's so funny?" Maria demanded.

"*You,*" Reggie gasped. "You should have seen your face when Geneva said that Gordon didn't have any food in his apartment." She started laughing again. "Geneva Clark is Gordon's twin sister."

Maria folded her arms and shot her a pointed look. "Why didn't you tell me?"

"I'm sorry about that," Reggie said. "But right before you came in, Geneva was complaining that everyone at this party considered her to be nothing more than Gordon Lewis's sister and that she was tired of being introduced that way."

"What about you and Gordon?" Elizabeth asked.

Reggie smiled brightly. "Well . . . it's still too early to know for sure, but I have a good feeling about us."

"All right!" Maria exclaimed.

Todd felt like a zombie when he arrived for his photo shoot with Quentin Berg on Friday morning. Although the bed in his apartment was an improvement over Ken's lumpy couch, Todd's neighbors had kept him awake all night. The shouting next door had continued until four A.M. Five minutes later country western music had started blaring from the apartment below his. *But I'm here on time,* Todd congratulated himself.

After his sessions with the makeup artist and hair stylist, Todd went to the wardrobe room to change into his first outfit for the day: bright orange moleskin pants topped with a royal blue velvet jacket and a paisley ascot tied at his throat. *What kind of guy would dress like this?* he asked himself incredulously.

Todd returned to the main area of the photography studio. Everyone was rushing around, preparing for the shoot. "Where's Simone?" Todd asked one of the technicians working the lights.

"Good question," the man replied. "She's lucky Quentin had a meeting this morning. But would you mind stepping just a few feet to the left? You're blocking our mark."

"Sorry," Todd mumbled.

He ambled over to the couch in the corner of the studio, where he wouldn't be in anyone's way.

An hour later Todd was still sitting there. Simone hadn't arrived yet, and Quentin had called to say that his meeting was running late. The whole crew was freaking out about being thrown off schedule. Todd wished he could take a long nap, but he knew he'd be in big trouble if he messed up his appearance.

Finally Simone strutted into the studio with her hand on her hip, looking very sexy in a skintight, shiny green jumpsuit and black leather boots. She struck a pose and pivoted in a complete circle, her black hair swirling around her face.

But watching her, Todd felt a slight twinge of disappointment. He recalled the delight of seeing

Elizabeth each morning at school . . . in the hall outside the *Oracle* office . . . at her locker. . . . *But Elizabeth isn't my girlfriend anymore,* he reminded himself with a swift mental kick. *Simone is.*

Todd rushed over to her, but before he could kiss her, she turned away.

"Time for that later," Simone said. "First, will someone please get me a mineral water!"

Just then Quentin and Jessica walked in, laughing at some inside joke.

Todd caught a glimpse of the sudden fierce look in Simone's eyes just before she grabbed him and planted a big, sloppy kiss on his lips. He tried to respond, but he was haunted by the suspicion that Simone was only putting on a show for Quentin and Jessica. The thought gave him a cold, hollow feeling in his gut.

When the kiss was over, Simone smiled sweetly at Todd and wiped a spot next to his mouth with her fingertips. "I think I've just messed up the makeup artist's hard work," she said, giggling.

Todd returned the smile, pushing aside his doubts. He didn't want to believe her affection was just an act. "I moved into my own apartment yesterday," he told her. "We'll be able to see each other whenever we want."

Simone wrapped her arms around his neck. "That's great, Todd."

He felt reassured by her reaction. "How about coming over for dinner tonight?" he suggested.

Jessica chuckled. "Quentin and I would love to come," she interjected, flashing Simone a catty look. "But we're already committed to another engagement."

"Well, *I* wouldn't miss dinner at your place for anything," Simone told Todd. "By the way, you look really hot in that suit. I think I'll buy it for you to wear next time we go out." Then she gave him another big kiss.

Sitting behind Leona's desk, Elizabeth waited for Gordon Lewis, who was due to arrive any second. She was wearing a pale gray skirt and matching vest with a pink, short-sleeved blouse. Elizabeth thought the outfit gave her a polished, professional image. *But what if Gordon takes one look at me and guesses I'm only sixteen?* she worried.

Elizabeth realized her hands were shaking. "Slow, deep breaths," she told herself, trying to calm her shaky nerves.

At the sound of the buzzer she jumped. Enid's voice came over the speaker. "Gordon Lewis is here to see you, Ms. Wakefield."

Elizabeth took one last calming breath. "Show him in, please," she answered. She dried her clammy palms on the front of her skirt and rose to her feet.

The moment the door opened, Elizabeth put on her best version of a self-confident smile. "Good morning, Gordon," she said, stepping out from behind the desk. "I'm so pleased to meet you at last." She shook his hand firmly.

Gordon raised his eyebrows in a look of mild surprise. "The pleasure is mine."

Elizabeth slipped behind the desk again and gestured toward the chair across from hers. "Please, have a seat. Would you like some coffee?"

Gordon sat down and linked his fingers across one knee. "Thanks, I would."

Elizabeth pressed the phone intercom button. "Enid, two coffees, please." She sat back and braced her elbows on the arms of the chair. "It'll just be a minute."

"You're much younger than I'd expected," Gordon commented.

Elizabeth chuckled good-naturedly. "Child prodigy," she replied. "That's what Leona calls me."

The door opened and Enid came in, carrying a tray with a pot of coffee, two china cups, spoons, cream, and sugar. Elizabeth thought she looked totally convincing as a secretary, wearing a dark blue dress and loose-fitting jacket, with a burgundy scarf draped around her neck.

After Enid served the coffee, she turned to Elizabeth and winked discreetly. "Will there be anything else, Ms. Wakefield?"

"Thanks, that'll do for now," Elizabeth answered.

"I'm surprised Leona hasn't approached me about this idea of yours," Gordon said, eyeing her over the rim of his coffee cup. "That is the usual way things are handled around here."

Elizabeth swallowed hard. "Yes, well . . . Leona

had some other matters to attend to and insisted I handle this project on my own."

Gordon seemed satisfied with her answer. Relieved, Elizabeth picked up the phone, pressed the numbers for Reggie's extension, and asked her to come in.

"He's there?" Reggie gasped.

Elizabeth smiled evenly. "And please bring the materials we went over this morning."

Reggie entered a moment later, carrying large boards with blown-up versions of the sample readers' columns Elizabeth had written. Even dressed in neutral colors—a dark brown silk blouse and skirt and a long tan jacket—Reggie seem to project a bright, colorful image.

Gordon smiled warmly as he shook Reggie's hand. Elizabeth noticed he held it a second longer than professional courtesy would require. "It's nice to see you again," he said.

Reggie nodded and smiled, as if she didn't trust herself to speak. She helped Elizabeth set up the boards, then took a seat next to Gordon.

Elizabeth briefly presented her idea. "'Free Style' would be a monthly column, selected from reader submissions. We'll announce a monthly theme in a prior issue and invite readers to share their thoughts on the subject." She glanced at Gordon Lewis, trying to gauge his reaction. He seemed to be listening attentively, but his serious, thoughtful expression gave no hint to his feelings.

"These are examples of what we expect to print," Elizabeth continued, pointing to her samples. "We want our readers to feel that *Flair* is their magazine, the source they turn to—and trust—for the latest fashion and beauty information. And the best way for us to develop loyal readership is to allow *them* to become part of *us*." She paused. "That's the reasoning behind 'Free Style.'"

Elizabeth finished making her presentation and turned to Gordon. Squeezing her hands together behind her back, she waited for him to say something. He was silent for a moment, and her heart started sinking. *He hates my idea,* she thought.

"I love it," Gordon said finally.

Elizabeth's eyes widened. "You do?" she squeaked. She cleared her throat. "I mean, I thought you would appreciate the concept."

"Absolutely," Gordon said. "And since it comes from you, who by all accounts represent the future of the fashion world, I'm sure it'll be a hit."

Elizabeth and Reggie exchanged victorious looks.

"There's a board meeting scheduled this afternoon at four o'clock," Gordon told them. "I'd like you both to be there." He shook hands with Elizabeth, then turned to Reggie. "Do you have a minute?" he asked.

"Sure," Reggie answered hesitatingly. She walked out of the office with him.

Elizabeth sat down heavily and closed her eyes. *We did it!* she realized. She was finally going to get the chance to present her idea to the board.

A moment later Reggie waltzed back in, her brown, almond-shaped eyes glittering. She closed the door and leaned back against it. "He asked me out for dinner Saturday night."

"That's fantastic!" Elizabeth cheered. She rushed over and gave Reggie a big hug. "But I'm not surprised," she added.

"At last my life is coming together," Reggie said dreamily.

"Jessica, where's my mineral water?" Simone screeched from the makeup table.

On the other side of the main studio area Jessica sighed wearily and brushed the sand off her hands. She was setting up a fake beach scene for the next layout and resented having to stop to cater to the impossible brat. But Simone's cries were too loud and shrill to ignore. She'd been in an especially nasty mood ever since Todd had left the studio a few hours earlier.

Jessica stepped out of the huge sandbox and went over to the cooler in a corner of the room. She'd stocked the cooler with mineral water and celery sticks in anticipation of Simone's constant demands. *I'll have to remember to treat my underlings with more class when I'm a supermodel,* she thought, squeezing the neck of a water bottle as if it were Simone's skinny white throat.

Shelly Fabian, the makeup artist, was an easygoing woman with smooth ebony skin, ample hips, and long skinny braids woven with colorful glass beads. She flashed a grateful smile as Jessica approached the table.

Simone was sitting with her legs stretched out in front of her, her arms folded tightly across her chest and her bottom lip curled in a sullen pout. Jessica thought she looked like a bad-tempered string bean. "Will there be anything else, Simone?" she asked, her voice dripping with sarcastic sweetness.

"I'll let you know," Simone replied snidely.

Shelly snorted. "Now, maybe I can get this eyeliner on your face before it goes out of style?"

Simone flashed her a nasty look, then grabbed the plastic bottle from Jessica's outstretched hand. "This is the wrong brand!" Simone complained, throwing the bottle on the floor. "Jessica, I know you're not the brightest kid in the world, but you can't be *that* dumb!"

Standing behind Simone, Shelly rolled her eyes.

Jessica stifled a giggle. "That was the only kind they had downstairs today."

"You're lying," Simone spat accusingly.

Jessica shrugged. "Call down to the cafeteria and ask them yourself if you don't believe me."

"Can I please get back to work?" Shelly asked impatiently, a cosmetic brush poised in her hand.

Simone pursed her lips and raised her chin. "No," she snapped. "Not until I get my mineral water."

"But the girl said they don't have it," Shelly argued, clearly losing her temper.

Simone sneered condescendingly. "This is a very big city. I'm sure they have my French mineral water *somewhere*. Go out and buy the *right* brand," she ordered Jessica. "And please try not to mess up again."

Quentin came over and gave Jessica a kiss on the cheek. "The beach set looks great," he commented. "You did a nice job. The red and blue towels were a perfect choice."

"Thanks," Jessica said, giving him a big smile. She glanced at Simone and was incredibly pleased with the look of pure venom in the model's eyes. Even though Jessica wasn't really in love with Quentin, she did love the effect their relationship had on Simone.

"OK, let's hurry up over here," Quentin said. "We're on a tight schedule this afternoon and already running late."

Simone crossed her arms and shot him a defiant look. "We're going to be running a whole lot later if Jessica doesn't figure out how to *read*, because I'm not moving from this chair until I have my mineral water."

Quentin exhaled loudly. "We don't have time for this, Simone," he warned. He turned to go.

"Well, I'm on a tight deadline too," Simone announced. "I need to get ready for my dinner with Todd, so you've got until four o'clock to finish this job."

Quentin stiffened. He turned around slowly, his eyes narrowed and shooting sparks at Simone. Jessica noticed Shelly moving away cautiously.

"What did you say?" Quentin demanded, his voice steady and cold.

"You heard me," Simone shot back.

A hush came over the studio. All work stopped. Jessica noticed the wary looks being exchanged among the crew members.

An angry red flush rose in Quentin's face. "OK, Simone. Have it your way. If you're in such a hurry, why don't get out of here *right now*?"

Simone blanched, obviously thrown off guard by his anger. "That's OK," she murmured defensively. "I signed on to do this shoot, and I'll do it."

"You don't understand," Quentin spat, emphasizing each word, "so let me make it clear. We won't be needing you after all, Simone."

Simone gaped at him, visibly alarmed. "But the shoot . . ."

"You're free to go, Simone," he stated evenly. "Jessica can do the shoot."

Yes, yes, yes! Jessica silently cheered.

"Quentin, I won't forget this . . . *ever*," Simone growled, her nostrils flaring.

"See that you don't," he replied smoothly.

Simone shot Jessica a look of pure loathing. Then she executed a perfect catwalk turn and stormed out of the studio.

Jessica watched her go, savoring the delicious victory. This was an even better break than she'd dared hope for!

"Back to work, everyone," Quentin barked. "Let's get you to wardrobe, Jessica."

"You bet!" Jessica replied eagerly, her heart leaping.

A short time later Jessica strutted into the main area of the studio, wearing a shimmering blue maillot with a long, diaphanous cover-up wrapped loosely around her hips. No one paid much attention to her except for a harried technician who called out to everyone that they were ready to begin the shoot.

Across the room someone replied, "Finally!"

Jessica was undaunted by everyone's apparent lack of appreciation. She'd studied her reflection in the dressing-room mirror and knew without a doubt that she looked totally fantastic. Filled with self-confidence, she made her way through the maze of equipment and cables to the beach set she'd helped create.

"All right!" Quentin cheered as he strolled into the studio. "Thanks to Jessica, we just might get this shoot finished in time. Who's working the breezes?" he asked.

A lanky, gray-haired technician jogged over with a small, battery-operated fan in his hand. "Right here, Quentin."

"Keep it soft to start," Quentin told him. "I want enough to flutter the hair around her face without pushing it back."

"You got it," the technician responded.

Quentin shot orders to the lighting crew, snapped his fingers at the guy operating the sound system, and winked at Jessica. "Let's begin!" he announced.

To the driving beat of techno music on CD, Jessica posed and preened for the camera. Quentin kept a running monologue going, directing her moves and calling for her to express various emotions as he snapped photo after photo. ". . . Now step to the left . . . sideways . . . flash me that gorgeous, sexy smile . . . and those eyes . . . I'm drowning in those ocean blue eyes. . . ." At one point his compliments were so outrageous, Jessica tipped her head back and burst out laughing.

"Beautiful!" Quentin exclaimed. "Laugh for me again, baby."

Jessica giggled, then whirled around and gave him a saucy look over her shoulder, her movements in sync with the music.

Quentin whistled. "You're beautiful!"

Jessica tucked her arms behind her back and tipped her head, letting the breeze from the fan blow her hair across her face. Quentin moved closer for a few shots, then slowly circled to the side of the sandbox for different angles.

This is what I was meant to do, Jessica realized. Modeling was more than fun. Being in front of the camera made her feel joyously alive, filled with pure energy. When Quentin called for a break, she was surprised to find that they'd been shooting for two solid hours, minus a few minutes here and there for wardrobe changes.

Quentin gave her a kiss on the cheek. "Good work, Jessica. I'm proud of you."

Then one of the crew members handed her a bottle of cold mineral water. Jessica realized it had come from the supply she'd brought in for Simone.

Jessica grinned, her whole body radiating with the glow of victory. *Look out, Simone!* she thought, raising the bottle in a silent toast to her absent archenemy. *I'm moving into your top spot.*

That afternoon Elizabeth and Reggie exchanged nervous glances as they sat at the long conference table, surrounded by the members of the editorial board. Elizabeth's heart was firmly lodged in her throat, and her whole body was shaking. Even the decor of the executive meeting room was imposing, with dark wood paneling on the walls and crystal chandeliers hanging from the ceiling.

Gordon stood at a podium at the head of the table, calling the meeting to order with an air of supreme authority. Elizabeth had been intimidated that morning when she'd faced him in Leona's office, but this was a million times worse. Everything about him shouted "power," from his dark pinstriped suit to his deep, steady voice. *What am I doing here?* Elizabeth thought, panic rising within her.

Gordon briefly introduced the idea of the reader column, then glanced at his watch. Obviously annoyed, he turned to Elizabeth. "It's after four-thirty. I don't know how much longer we can wait for Leona."

Elizabeth gulped. "Leona?"

"You did inform her of this meeting?" he asked, pinning Elizabeth with a sharp look.

Elizabeth nodded, her eyes wide. "Yes . . . but Leona had an emergency to take care of this afternoon," she improvised. "She said she'd try to get back in time for the meeting, but if not, we should go ahead and present the proposal to the board." Elizabeth held her breath, waiting for his next move. *What if he throws us out of the meeting?* she worried.

But Gordon seemed to accept the explanation. He introduced Elizabeth and Reggie, then turned the meeting over to them.

Elizabeth felt strangely lightheaded as she and Reggie stepped up to the podium. The reality of the situation pressed down on her with terrible force. Her legs were like rubber, her throat dry, and for one long, horrifying moment, her mind went completely blank.

Then Reggie discreetly pinched her arm, and the stinging pain jolted Elizabeth out of her daze. "Good afternoon," she said, her voice trembling slightly. "I'm here to tell you about 'Free Style,' an exciting new concept for increasing *Flair* readership through maximized reader loyalty."

As Elizabeth gave an overview of her idea, her confidence increased. It gratified her to see the attentive expressions around the table. The sample columns and promotional copy she'd written seemed to go over particularly well. "'Free Style' will be the bridge between the real woman and the fashion fantasy," Elizabeth declared, her voice clear and strong now. "But of course, a new idea must also be measured by its bottom-line projections." She turned the presentation over to Reggie.

"We fashion editors face a daunting challenge in presenting today's look to today's woman," Reggie began, gripping the sides of the podium. "Reader loyalty is our strongest weapon in a fiercely competitive market. We estimate 'Free Style' will increase *Flair* readership by twenty to thirty percent over the first three years of implementation." Reggie paused. "But unlike other promotional programs, 'Free Style' will utilize resources that are currently available or that can be acquired with minimum expense."

Elizabeth felt giddy with relief when the presentation was over. She and Reggie thanked the board members for their time and offered to answer any of their questions or concerns about "Free Style."

"I think this is a marvelous project," one woman commented. "Have you considered targeting various age ranges of readers?"

"No, we haven't," Elizabeth replied. "But that's a good idea. It would be interesting to look at a similar theme from the thirty-year-old, twenty-year-old, and teen points of view."

Others offered their opinions and suggestions, and a lively conversation developed around the table. It was obvious that "Free Style" was a hit. Elizabeth felt a rush of pleasure swelling inside her. *The editorial board of L.A.'s hottest fashion magazine is discussing* my *idea,* she marveled to herself.

"I think we're ready to go for a vote on this

matter," Gordon said, stepping up to the podium.

Elizabeth held her breath. *It's really happening!* she thought. She glanced at Reggie, who smiled back with a look of excited anticipation in her eyes.

Suddenly the double doors flew open. Elizabeth turned to see what had happened—and froze, her heart in her throat.

Leona was standing in the doorway, braced with crutches, her brown eyes flashing with rage.

Chapter 5

A hush fell over the conference table as Leona limped into the room. Despite the crutches she looked as sharp and polished as usual, in a short-skirted herringbone suit with black suede trim. A taupe silk blouse, gold knot earrings, and a gold chain necklace complemented the outfit. Her hair was impeccably arranged in a sleek, straight style, not a single dark blond strand out of place.

Leona was dressed for battle.

What is she doing here? Elizabeth wondered. A cold feeling of dread enveloped her, weighing her down until she felt as if she might sink into the plush gray carpet under her feet. Next to her Reggie uttered a soft groan.

"Sorry I'm late," Leona stated evenly as she lowered herself into a chair at the end of the table.

Gordon stared at her incredulously. "What happened? Were you in an accident?"

"Yes, but lucky for me I'm back in time for this meeting." She fixed Elizabeth with a piercing glare.

Elizabeth swallowed hard and lowered her eyes. *How did Leona find out?* she wondered.

"We're just about to vote on the proposal for 'Free Style,'" Gordon told Leona. "Your child prodigy has handled the presentation admirably," he added.

"My child prodigy?" Leona shrieked. "Not in this lifetime! After all I've done for you, Elizabeth! How could you turn on me like this?"

Elizabeth gulped. She wanted to say something in her own defense, but her throat felt like stone. All she could do was shake her head mutely.

Leona turned to Reggie. "And you! You're never going to get away with this! You can kiss your career good-bye. I'll see to it that you never work in fashion editing again."

Gordon raised his hands, his expression grave. "You'd better explain yourself, Leona," he demanded.

"That girl is an *intern!*" Leona responded, pointing at Elizabeth. "She's a high-school kid and a conniving, no-good thief. With Reggie's help she stole *my* idea for 'Free Style'—along with most of my proposal."

"These are very serious accusations," Gordon challenged. "You'd better have proof."

"Of course I have proof," Leona replied. "Memos, copies, computer files—I have tons of documentation."

All of it false! Elizabeth's mind screamed.

"*You* stole the idea from Elizabeth," Reggie accused hotly.

Leona shot her a withering look. "Is that what she told you?" She uttered a quick, nasty laugh. "Elizabeth seems to be an accomplished liar. She managed to fool me and apparently everyone else," she said, gazing at the others around the table.

Facing the icy stares of the board members, Elizabeth opened her mouth to protest, but only a strangled sound came up from her throat.

Gordon looked directly at Reggie, his blue eyes filled with accusation. "You knew Elizabeth was an intern," he charged.

Reggie nodded solemnly. "But I can explain—"

"Never mind," he said tersely, cutting her off. "The situation is painfully clear."

"Gordon, if you'd only hear me out," Reggie pleaded.

His expression hardened. "This meeting is adjourned. You're both fired. I'll phone security and have them send someone up to escort you out of the building."

Elizabeth reeled back as if she'd been socked in the face. Her legs felt unsteady, and bright colors swirled before her eyes. She clutched the back of a chair to keep from crumpling into a heap on the carpet.

I was so close, Elizabeth thought, her heart sinking. But she felt even worse for Reggie, whose dream of finally being with Gordon seemed shattered beyond hope.

*　　　*　　　*

Todd swiped the back of his hand across his sweaty forehead as he scanned the directions on the box of scalloped potatoes mix. "Where am I going to get a two-quart casserole pan?" he wondered aloud, frustrated.

Todd desperately wanted this dinner to turn out perfect. He'd invited his parents and Simone and was eager to prove to all three that he could make it on his own. He'd bought a ton of groceries and a cookbook and had spent hours preparing the main course—marinated pork roast with garlic and peppercorns.

With the roast baking in the oven, Todd was concentrating on the side dishes. "A two-quart casserole, huh?" he grumbled. "Let's see what we've got." He knelt in front of the cavernous bottom cupboard and searched through the kitchen paraphernalia that had come with the apartment. "What junk!" he muttered, pulling out a greasy, stained plastic bowl. He found a bread pan with a hole rusted through the bottom, tons of mangled spoons and forks, assorted parts to an electric coffeepot, and a mass of tangled extension cords—but nothing even close to a two-quart casserole pan.

Todd noticed everything in the cupboard was sprinkled with what looked like black grains of wild rice or caraway seeds. *I guess a gourmet slob used to live here,* he thought.

As he was tossing the stuff back into the cupboard he smelled something burning. "What the—," he began, springing to his feet. A veil of smoke was seeping out from around the oven door.

"My roast!" he moaned. Todd reached for the chrome handle on the oven door, which was as hot as a sizzling frying pan. "Ouch!" he yelped, jerking his hand away. He grabbed a thick wad of paper towels to use as a makeshift potholder and yanked the oven door open.

Clouds of smoke billowed out, choking him. Todd held his breath as he lifted the smoldering pan out of the oven and dumped the whole thing into the sink. The tender, juicy, flavorful pork roast of his dreams had turned into a shriveled-up, smoldering black lump.

"No problem," Todd told himself, trying to pretend he was calm. He went around the apartment, opening all the windows to let in some fresh air. So he'd change the menu; big deal. *To what?* he wondered.

Todd returned to the kitchen and surveyed the contents of his refrigerator. He'd thoroughly washed the interior before putting away the groceries, but the faint odor of sour milk still lingered. "Chicken," Todd said, sighing with relief. He'd bought a stuffed, precooked chicken that only needed to be heated for twenty minutes. It even came with its own disposable baking pan. *Am I prepared or what?* Todd mentally congratulated himself.

Todd peeled off the plastic wrapper. He figured after the chicken was done, he could use the same pan for the scalloped potatoes. *My dinner is saved,* he thought. He popped the chicken into the oven, then set about to clean up the evidence of his pork disaster.

After dumping the roast into the garbage, Todd tried to wash out the pan. The black gunk that coated the bottom was baked on solid. He was tempted to throw the pan away too, but it had come with the apartment. Todd's lease specified that if anything was missing when he moved out, he'd have to forfeit part of his security deposit.

Todd decided to let the pan soak for a few days, hoping some of the mess would dissolve. But he didn't want to leave it in the sink where his parents would see it.

After considering several hiding places, Todd carried the pan into his bedroom and pushed it under his bed. While he was there, he noticed more of the black sprinkles he'd found in the kitchen. *That's strange,* he thought. He picked up a few between his fingers and spread them out on his palm for a closer look.

Todd suddenly realized what they actually were. Disgusted, he shook his hand vigorously. "This place is covered with mice droppings!" He groaned as he rushed into the bathroom to scrub his hands.

A few minutes later, as he was changing into a clean pair of jeans and shirt, Todd realized that the odor of burned food was still pretty strong, even with all the windows open. Actually it seemed to be getting *worse.*

He stopped in the middle of buttoning his shirt and sniffed the air. "No!" he shouted, bolting out of the room. "Not my chicken too!"

Again the kitchen was filled with dense gray clouds. Holding his arm across his face to cover his nose and mouth, Todd groped his way to the stove. When he opened the oven, gusts of pungent smoke billowed out.

Todd dumped the smoldering chicken into the sink and turned on the faucet. "Now what?" he cried, totally discouraged. Obviously there was something wrong with the oven—which meant the scalloped potatoes were off the list too. That seriously limited his options for dinner.

He waved a damp towel in the air to move the smoke toward the open kitchen window. Then he searched through his stock of food for something else to cook. He'd wanted to serve something fancy, impressive—but it seemed his choices were limited to buttered toast, canned soup, macaroni and cheese, or peanut butter and jelly.

He settled for macaroni and cheese and toast. *Pasta and bread won't be so bad,* Todd assured himself. After all, lots of fancy restaurants served meals that were basically nothing more than pasta and bread.

Preparing the toast was a bit tricky because the old toaster didn't push the bread up when it was done. The first slices he tried added more smoke to the gray haze that still lingered at the ceiling. He had to watch over the toast as it browned, then pull it out with wooden tongs.

Todd dragged the small kitchen table into the living room and set it with the mismatched plastic plates and cups he'd found in the cupboards. After he laid out the food, he stood back and frowned. "This is pathetic," he said.

He considered running down to the gas station on the corner to use the pay phone to call out for pizza or Chinese food. But at that moment the doorbell rang. Todd gulped. It was too late to change the menu.

This is it, he thought, bracing himself as he opened the door. His parents were standing there . . . and right behind them was Simone.

Lying in a patio chair in her backyard, Elizabeth felt totally drained. Scenes from her disaster that day kept flashing through her mind: images of Leona's rage . . . accusing looks from the board members . . . Gordon Lewis's cold expression as he'd called for a security officer to escort Elizabeth and Reggie from the building. . . .

But worst of all was the visible heartbreak on Reggie's face. Elizabeth squeezed her eyes shut and groaned softly. No matter how much it hurt, her brain kept rehashing the horror of those final minutes of the board meeting.

At first she'd been in a state of shock. During the bus ride home from Los Angeles that afternoon, she'd felt completely numb. The depression had set in a short time later, pressing down on Elizabeth as though she were carrying a ton of granite on her head.

Elizabeth shifted her position in the chair and gazed absently into the crystal blue water of her family's pool. She'd come outside that evening with the intention of swimming laps, hoping the exercise would help stop the mental torture for a while. But now she couldn't force herself to move from the chair. She had no energy for swimming. She wondered if she'd have enough to get herself back into the house.

I lost everything, Elizabeth realized. Not only had her plan backfired, destroying her career opportunities at *Flair* and at every other magazine owned by Mode, but she'd also ruined the life of her only friend in the company. *Poor Reggie would've been better off if she'd never met me,* Elizabeth thought sadly.

"Hey, Liz!" Jessica called as she bounded outside and ran over to her twin. "You'll never guess what happened today. I—yes, me, Jessica Wakefield—will be appearing in a huge swimsuit layout in next month's issue of *Flair!*"

She plunked herself into a lawn chair and scooted it closer to Elizabeth. "It was fabulous!" Jessica gushed, leaning back and kicking her legs in the air. "I can see why everyone thinks Quentin is such great photographer." She bolted upright and giggled. "Because he really is. He's a great artist, but he also makes the work fun. He had me laughing. . . ." She sighed dreamily.

Elizabeth forced herself to smile.

"But that's not the best part," Jessica added. "Guess

why I'm going to be in the layout—instead of Simone."

Elizabeth shrugged. "Haven't got a clue."

Jessica crossed her legs and grinned smugly. "Simone was acting like the biggest brat in the whole world today, worse than usual. She came in *hours* late, for starters, wearing a green satin jumpsuit that looked like it had been painted on. Then after lunch, while the rest of us were working our heads off to get everything set up for the shoot, she decided that mineral water from Maine wasn't good enough for her."

Seems Simone's day was almost as bad as mine, Elizabeth thought dryly as her twin filled her in on the details of her victory.

"It was so wonderful, Liz," Jessica said. "Quentin just kicked her out and put me in. Then she stormed off in a huff, and I swear, her skin looked as green as her outfit! He's taking me to a celebrity party at Planet Hollywood tonight," she added excitedly.

"That's great, Jess," Elizabeth responded, genuinely pleased that things had worked out so well for her twin.

"This internship is turning out better than I'd dreamed," Jessica declared. "But the best part of it is that you and I are doing it together."

Elizabeth exhaled a shaky breath. "Together," she repeated.

"Wouldn't it be wonderful if you and I both ended up working at *Flair* permanently?" Jessica asked dreamily.

Elizabeth caught her bottom lip between her teeth as she tried to control the flood of despair washing over her. But her sister's words had broken down the last of her defenses.

Powerless to stop herself, Elizabeth burst into tears.

Jessica was startled by Elizabeth's sudden reaction. "Liz, what's wrong?" she asked. "Is it Todd?" *Did that jerk do something else to twist the knife in her back?* she wondered hotly.

Elizabeth opened her mouth as if to speak, but she was sobbing too hard to answer.

Jessica reached across the gap that separated their chairs and hugged her sister. "He's not worth it, Liz," she whispered soothingly as she patted her twin's back. "Believe me, dating Simone is the perfect punishment for a guy who—"

Elizabeth shook her head. "No, not Todd," she sobbed.

Jessica leaned back and looked at her directly. "What is it, then?"

"Everything!" Elizabeth wailed. "I got fired."

Jessica's jaw dropped. "From *Flair?*" she asked in disbelief.

Elizabeth nodded as a flood of fresh tears streamed down her face.

"Why? What happened?"

Elizabeth drew a shaky breath. "It all started with an idea I'd had for the magazine . . . ," she began.

Jessica's reactions went from concern to bewilderment to pure hot anger as she listened to her sister's story. "Leona Peirson actually took your idea and passed it off as her own?" she raged.

Elizabeth nodded. "I might have never known about it if I hadn't listened to the tape recorder I found in her condo."

Jessica raised her eyebrows. "Her condo?"

Elizabeth laced her fingers around her raised knee. "Leona asked me to take care of her personal errands while she was recuperating in Lake Tahoe. She keeps a spare set of keys in her office."

Jessica exhaled sharply. "Leona stabs you in the back, then expects you to be her *maid?* What a snake!" she cried.

Elizabeth's lips twitched as if she were trying to smile. "That's exactly what I think of her." She went on to explain how she, Enid, Maria, and Reggie Andrews had tried to get back at Leona. "But the whole thing fell apart when she burst into the board meeting this afternoon," Elizabeth said, choking back a sob.

"How did Leona know you and Reggie would be there?" Jessica asked.

Elizabeth shrugged weakly. "I wondered that myself. But I guess it doesn't matter now."

"It's so *unfair!*" Jessica exclaimed. "That witch should've been the one to get fired—not you!"

Elizabeth sniffed. "*Fair* doesn't seem to mean much in the world of high-fashion publishing." She brushed the back of her hand across her damp cheek. "We gave it our best shot, though. I'm just sorry I've ruined Reggie's life in the process."

"Your plan wasn't half bad," Jessica admitted, impressed with her twin's daring creativity. "But you should've come to *me* in the first place." She gently squeezed Elizabeth's hand. "Enid and Maria may be good friends, but trust me—they're not too swift when it comes to being devious and manipulative. Those are *my* specialties."

Elizabeth sniffed and cracked a slight grin. "I'll keep that in mind."

"You do that," Jessica replied.

"I'm just glad it's over," Elizabeth breathed.

Jessica squeezed her bottom lip between her teeth. *No, it isn't over—not by a long shot,* she vowed to herself. *Leona Peirson is going to get exactly what she deserves.*

After all the times her older sister had come to her rescue, Jessica decided it was her turn to do the same for Elizabeth.

Chapter 6

"Did you enjoy working in Paris?" Todd's mother asked Simone during dinner.

Simone wrinkled her nose at the food on her plate. "Not really," she answered without looking up. "What's in this orange slop?"

Todd breathed an exasperated sigh. "I already told you," he reminded her. "Macaroni and cheese."

"It's very creamy," Mrs. Wilkins commented. "What brand did you use?"

Simone rolled her eyes and mumbled something under her breath.

Todd cringed, then turned to his mother. "I'm not sure what kind I bought," he answered. He'd already thrown away the box. And besides, he knew his mother had only asked to be polite.

"I think I'll have more of this toast," Mr. Wilkins announced as he added a few more slices to his plate. "It's delicious. Just the right amount of butter." When he tried to pass the serving platter to Simone, she waved it aside.

"Oh, please!" she whined, fingering the stiff collar of her bright blue dress. "The day I resort to eating buttered toast . . ." She didn't finish the sentence, but her sentiments were clear—she'd have to be desperate to eat the meal Todd had prepared.

Todd admitted to himself that the dinner was an unqualified disaster. His parents were trying too hard to be gracious, and Simone had been wearing a look of utter disgust since the moment she'd first walked into the apartment. Todd's one lucky break was that his shouting neighbors weren't home.

"I must admit buttered toast is one of my weaknesses," Mrs. Wilkins said, helping herself to another piece. "What are your favorite foods, Simone?"

Simone braced her elbows on the table, her hands under her chin. "Carrots, celery . . . I stick to fresh vegetables most of the time," she replied in a haughty tone. "Even if I weren't a top model, I'd still watch my weight. There's no excuse for a woman letting herself go."

Todd hadn't considered that she might be referring to his mother—until Simone turned to Emily Wilkins with a snide look and added, "No offense."

A bright red flush rose in his mother's face, her deep green eyes simmering. For a long, tense moment no one said a word. Todd shifted uneasily in his seat. The only person who didn't seemed to be in a state of shock was Simone. She studied her fingernails, which were painted the same blue shade as her dress. Finally Bert Wilkins broke the silence. "So Todd, are getting yourself settled in?" he asked.

Todd shrugged. "I want to fix up the place a little."

"That would be nice," Emily Wilkins commented, pushing her short auburn hair behind her ear. "Some fresh paint . . . maybe a few colorful throw rugs . . ."

Simone snorted loudly. "A bulldozer would be your best bet."

"I know this isn't the best apartment in the world, Simone," Todd responded defensively. "I'm planning to move to a nicer place as soon as I can afford to."

"I'll visit you when that happens, Todd," Simone replied coldly as she got up from the table. "But in the meantime this place is giving me the creeps." She pushed her fingers through her short dark hair, then lowered her hand to her hip. With her shoulders pressed back, hips jutted forward, and nose stuck in the air, Simone sauntered out of the apartment, slamming the door behind her.

Todd lowered his eyes, his face burning with humiliation as he and his parents sat in awkward silence. Again it was his father who spoke first. "Simone seems like a spirited girl," he remarked.

Mrs. Wilkins smiled wryly. "She certainly is."

Todd felt the macaroni and cheese sitting heavily in his stomach. He knew his parents were trying to show their support for him, even though it was obvious that he'd made a huge mistake—*several* huge mistakes.

Todd absently chewed off a corner of cold, greasy toast. *Man, do I miss Elizabeth!* he admitted silently. He decided it was time to tell Elizabeth the truth— that he still loved her and probably always would.

But before Todd could go to Elizabeth and beg her to forgive him, he first needed to break things off with Simone.

In the middle of the night Elizabeth was jostled from a deep sleep. She opened her eyes and saw her sister's shadowy form standing over her bed.

"The keys," Jessica whispered urgently, shaking Elizabeth's shoulders. "Wake up!"

"Stop it," Elizabeth groaned. Jessica shook her harder, nearly rattling her twin's teeth.

"All right, I'm awake!" Elizabeth muttered in self-defense. She sat up and pushed her hair back from her face. "What's wrong?"

"What did you do with Leona's keys?" Jessica asked.

Elizabeth exhaled wearily and glanced at the lighted digital display on her clock radio. "It's two o'clock in the morning," she whined.

Jessica sat down on the edge of the mattress. "Do you still have Leona's keys?"

Elizabeth nodded, yawning. "I never got around to putting them back in her desk."

"Yes!" Jessica cheered softly.

"Can I go back to sleep now?" Elizabeth grumbled as she lowered her head to her pillow.

"No way. Get up and put these on," Jessica ordered, dumping a few articles of clothing on Elizabeth's face.

Elizabeth shoved them aside and sat up again. "Maybe you should tell me what's going on, Jess."

"I've come up with a brilliant plan that might help prove the magazine idea was yours. But we really have to hurry," Jessica urged. "I'll fill you in about the details on the way."

Twenty minutes later Elizabeth was sitting in the passenger seat of the twins' Jeep, staring incredulously at her sister as they headed along the interstate toward L.A. "*That's* your brilliant plan, Jess? To sneak into Leona's condo and steal her tape recorder?"

Jessica shrugged. "Sure, why not? That tape is what clued you in to Leona's dirty dealing in the first place. Maybe when Gordon Lewis listens to it, he'll have a few doubts about her himself."

"I should have guessed," Elizabeth muttered, glancing at the black jeans and sweatshirt her twin had ordered her to wear. Jessica was dressed the same, and two black ski masks and four black leather gloves lay in a single heap between their seats.

Jessica shifted lanes to pass a slow-moving van. "What other choice do we have?" she asked.

"I don't care," Elizabeth replied tersely. "Turn around at the next exit because we aren't going through with it. Breaking and entering is a serious crime."

"You're absolutely right about that," Jessica said breezily. "But thanks to you and Leona's keys, we won't be *breaking* and entering—just entering."

"I think it's called 'illegal trespassing,'" Elizabeth retorted.

"Leona Peirson *invited* you to let yourself into the condo, right?" Jessica said.

Elizabeth folded her arms. "What's your point?" she asked wryly.

"Well," Jessica began, "Leona never actually *uninvited* you, did she?"

Elizabeth glared at her. "Jessica, she *fired* me."

Jessica shrugged. "It's not the same thing," she countered.

"It's close enough." Elizabeth turned toward the window and stared into the darkness. She thought back to Thursday afternoon, when she'd played the tape for Enid and Maria in Leona's condo. *Why didn't I grab it when I had the chance?* she wondered, mentally kicking herself.

"How can you possibly sit back and do nothing?" Jessica demanded. "Leona Peirson stabbed you in the back, and you're the one who's going to have to pay for it, Liz."

Elizabeth absently toyed with a loose thread on her sleeve. "I just want to put it behind me," she said tiredly.

"What about your plans of getting a summer job at *Flair*, maybe working as an editor someday?" Jessica asked pointedly. "Do you want to put all that behind you too?"

"I don't know." Elizabeth leaned her head back and sighed. "Having that tape might help clear my name, but it's so risky. . . ."

Jessica smiled broadly. "It would be so easy to sneak into her condo and get it. Leona wouldn't even know we were there." She giggled. "And even if she did wake up, she can't exactly chase us down on crutches."

Elizabeth nervously chewed her bottom lip. "It's totally crazy."

"Look at it this way. . . . What if you'd left your backpack at Leona's, with your all your school stuff," Jessica began. "And let's say you had a very important test tomorrow and you absolutely needed your books. Leona is sound asleep with a broken leg, and you have her keys."

Jessica tipped her head questioningly. "Would you rudely wake Leona up and ask for your bag, or would you politely let yourself into her condo and get the bag without bothering her?"

Elizabeth frowned, bemused. "I have no idea what you're talking about," she said.

"Pretend the tape recorder is your backpack and we don't want to disturb Leona while she's sleeping," Jessica explained breezily.

Elizabeth rolled her eyes, amazed at how far her twin's logic could stretch. "The tape recorder might not still be on the side table."

"It's worth a look," Jessica insisted.

Elizabeth pictured the side table in the living

room where she'd left the tape recorder. It wasn't too far from the front door, only five or six feet . . . just a few quick steps . . . a matter of seconds. . . . Elizabeth stiffened, shocked at the direction of her thoughts.

Then she recalled how devastated she'd been when Gordon Lewis had called security to have her and Reggie escorted from the Mode building. And she remembered Reggie's miserable expression. . . . Elizabeth squeezed her eyes shut and took a deep, shaky breath.

Jessica drummed her fingers on the steering wheel. "We're only minutes from L.A.," she pointed out. "It would be a shame to have come all this way for nothing."

Maybe if Gordon heard Leona's tape, he'd understand why Reggie helped me and would forgive her, Elizabeth thought. She caught her bottom lip between her teeth and gazed out the window. "Jessica, take the Ocean Lane exit and turn left at the first light," she whispered.

"All right, sis!" Jessica cheered.

Elizabeth nervously wrung her hands together, her stomach flipping and turning. *We have to at least try to get back that tape,* she reasoned. *There's no other choice.*

Chapter 7

When the twins arrived at Leona's condominium complex, Elizabeth was dismayed to see how well lighted the area was. Floodlights shone over the entrance to the main driveway, as if standing guard against trespassers. Ground lamps seemed to have been planted everywhere else.

But the cherry trees that surrounded the complex provided a solid trail of shadows. *This will work,* Elizabeth thought, willing herself to feel strong and confident—despite the nervous fluttering in her gut and the squeezing sensation in her throat.

Wearing black ski masks and gloves, the twins followed the shadows of the cherry trees around to Leona's building. The windows of her condo unit were completely dark. Elizabeth hoped it meant that Leona was sound asleep.

Elizabeth clenched her fist around Leona's keys to

keep them from jingling as she and Jessica stalked up to her second-floor condo. *This will work,* Elizabeth chanted over and over. She unlocked Leona's door and pushed it open, holding her breath. Jessica squeezed her hand as they tiptoed into the foyer.

Jessica kept watch at the entrance to the hallway that led to Leona's bedroom while Elizabeth slipped into the living room and carefully picked her steps toward the seating arrangement. Pale moonlight shone through the glass panels on the far wall, allowing her to make out the shapes of some of the furniture and miscellaneous objects among the shadows in the room.

Feeling her way with her hand along the back of the couches, Elizabeth located the side table. Immediately her fingers curled around a small, rectangular object. Elizabeth sighed with relief. Crouching down next to the table, she took out her flashlight and risked a quick peek to see that the tape was still in the tape recorder.

Yes! she silently cheered. Anxious to get away with her prize, Elizabeth hurried toward the doorway.

But as she crossed the room Elizabeth tripped over an unexpected suitcase lying on the floor and fell flat on her face with a heavy thud. Still clutching the tape recorder, she froze.

Suddenly Jessica was there, dragging her up by the arm. "Leona's coming!" she hissed.

Elizabeth's heart jumped to her throat. She grasped Jessica's hand and whispered, "Out the back!" They dashed into the kitchen, where a small light above the sink had been left on. The clop-thud pattern of footsteps sounded from the foyer. *Leona's right behind us!* Elizabeth's mind screamed. Gripped with panic, she raced to the sliding glass doors that opened to the second-floor deck. Her hand shook uncontrollably as she fumbled with the latch.

"Hurry!" Jessica urged.

Elizabeth tugged on the door, but it wouldn't budge. The clop-thud footsteps moved into the living room, drawing closer.

Elizabeth uttered a strangled groan from deep in her throat. Then Jessica crouched down and reached for a brass latch near the bottom of the door that Elizabeth hadn't noticed.

As the twins rushed outside, several outdoor lamps flashed on. The entire deck, including the stairs to the ground level, was caught in the bright, glaring light.

"This way," Jessica hissed. She swung her leg over the railing and lowered herself down the other side.

She'll break her neck! Elizabeth worried as she watched her twin shinnying down one of the support posts. Then she heard a sound at the door. In the space of a heartbeat Elizabeth shoved the tape recorder into her back pocket and leaped over the deck railing herself.

Gripping the post with her arms and legs, she inched downward. When her feet finally touched the ground, she and Jessica dove into the shadows.

Elizabeth glanced back and saw Leona standing on her deck, wearing a long white satin robe that shone in the light. Elizabeth's heart stopped for an instant, then she and Jessica took off running.

When they finally reached the Jeep, a Doberman pinscher with a bloodthirsty gleam in his eyes was standing next to it, blocking their path. The girls stopped for a moment, then gingerly stepped closer.

"Nice puppy," Elizabeth cooed, holding out her hand to let him sniff it.

The beast bared his teeth and growled.

"This is totally ridiculous," Jessica declared. She waved her fist at the dog and growled back. "We don't have time for this, so beat it!" she commanded.

To Elizabeth's surprise, the Doberman ducked his head and skulked away.

"What a way to start the weekend!" Jessica exclaimed as they jumped into the Jeep. She pulled off her ski mask and laughed. "We even had a wild animal to spice up the adventure. Do you think Leona recognized us?"

Elizabeth gulped. "I hope not." She peeled off her own mask and shook out her matted hair.

Jessica started the engine and headed back toward the interstate. "OK, let's check out the prize," she said. "I want to hear the tape."

Elizabeth pressed the play button and adjusted the volume. Leona's crisp, all-business voice filled the cab of the Jeep. Recognizing the letter to the head of marketing, Elizabeth fast forwarded the tape for a second, then let it resume playing.

"Letter to Jonah Hall, advertising," Leona was saying.

Elizabeth frowned. The incriminating memo that referred to her should have followed Leona's letter to the marketing department. "It's gone!" she cried. "The letter to Gordon about 'Free Style' isn't here anymore. Leona taped over it!"

"Let's listen to the whole tape," Jessica suggested. "Maybe you don't have the right place."

"No," Elizabeth argued. "I remember exactly where it was, right after the letter to Rupert Perry in marketing."

"Are you positive?" Jessica asked.

Elizabeth nodded, tears pooling in her eyes. "I guess it's really over now. Without that memo I don't have any evidence against Leona—and no hope of proving my innocence."

Todd knocked on the door of Simone's apartment Saturday afternoon, feeling confident that he'd made the right decision. They didn't belong together at all. If he'd needed any more proof of that fact, all he had to do was remember last night's dinner.

The door flew open and a tall, thin girl with bright red hair came bounding out, nearly bumping into him.

"Oh, hi!" she gushed, her blue-green eyes wide with surprise.

Todd realized that the girl's eyes were the same color as Elizabeth's, and a sharp, longing pain sliced through him. "I'm here to see Simone," he told her.

"I'm her roommate, Cecile," the girl said.

Todd nodded. He remembered speaking to her over the phone when he'd tried to reach Simone a few days earlier.

"Sorry I have to rush off," Cecile said, already stepping away as she spoke. "Simone's on the phone, but go in and make yourself comfy."

Todd thanked her and entered the apartment. Following the sound of Simone's voice, he walked into a huge living room with a high ceiling and lots of windows. Simone was sitting on the floor, leaning back against a pile of large cushions in a corner. She was wearing bright pink boxer shorts that showed off her long, shapely legs and a white cropped T-shirt that showed off quite a bit too.

"Todd, *darling*," she gushed loudly, clamping her hand loosely over the telephone mouthpiece. "It's so great to see you. I was getting so lonesome. Kick off your shoes and get comfy." She blew him a pouty kiss. "I'll meet you on that nice, soft couch in just a second—as soon as I finish taking care of a little business matter."

Todd shifted uneasily as she resumed her phone conversation. He suspected this wasn't going to be as easy as he'd hoped. Feeling incredibly out of place, he paced around the room, tapping his fingers against the sides of his thighs.

He'd never been in Simone's apartment before. Todd wondered how long it would take before he could afford something as nice. Her living room alone was more than twice the size of his place.

Todd tried not to eavesdrop on Simone's conversation, but she was practically screaming into the phone. He quickly realized she was talking to Quentin and that their "business matter"—whatever it was—wasn't going too well.

"Yes, that's right—Todd!" Simone was saying. "Todd is here. I'm thrilled. And no one cares what *you* think about it!"

Todd cringed. He didn't like the sound of that at all. The last thing he needed was to have Quentin mad at him. Without the support of the famous photographer, Todd knew his chances of making it big as a fashion model were dismal. He could be stuck in his dank, disgusting apartment, living with rodents and cockroaches, for a long time.

Simone cursed, then uttered a bitter laugh. "Yeah? Well, I think *you're* a dirty, rotten, scum-of-the-earth jerk!"

She slammed down the phone. "Quentin Berg can be such a creep."

Todd didn't know how to reply, so he simply shrugged.

Simone stood up and pushed her hands through her hair. The motion caused her T-shirt to slip higher, revealing more of her smooth white skin.

Todd stared at her blankly. Everything about

Simone—her body, her clothes, her expressions, the way she moved—was incredibly sexy. But seeing her now, Todd was surprised to realize that he felt absolutely no attraction to her.

Simone jutted her hip sideways and looped her thumbs into the waistband of her boxers. "You're standing there like you're ready to bolt," she pouted.

Todd rubbed his hand across the back of his neck. "Actually," he began, "I'm sort of in a hurry—"

"I'm really glad you're here," she interrupted, flashing him a sweet smile. "Now sit down, kick off your shoes, and relax. I'll be right back."

"No, wait," he protested.

Simone giggled. "I love it when you're eager. Don't worry, I'll just be two seconds." She disappeared through a set of swinging double doors, leaving him feeling utterly exasperated.

Maybe I should've broken up with her in a letter, Todd grumbled to himself as he sat on the edge of the couch. He glanced down at the toes of his basketball sneakers. *And I'm definitely keeping my shoes on!*

Nearly twenty minutes went by before Simone returned, carrying a tray of raw carrot sticks, two cartons of low-fat yogurt, and a large bottle of mineral water. "Here we are, sweetheart," she announced. "Lunch." She set the tray on the coffee table in front of the couch.

"Looks filling," Todd muttered sarcastically.

Simone giggled. "It's what models eat, Todd. Join the club."

"Thanks, Simone, uh . . . I didn't come here for lunch," he muttered awkwardly.

Simone snuggled up next to him on the couch. "I know, but it's the least I could do after you went to the trouble of preparing a home-cooked dinner last night." She leaned forward and picked up a carrot stick. "I had such a good time. Your parents are really nice," she added sweetly.

Todd gaped at her, bewildered by her sudden change of attitude. She had to be one of the weirdest girls he'd ever known. *Why was I even attracted to her in the first place?* he wondered. He remembered thinking she was gorgeous, an exotic combination of pale skin and black hair, with luscious full lips and a long, lean body. But now, watching her gnaw on the tip of a carrot stick with her pointy front teeth, she reminded him of a rodent. *She's freaky looking,* he thought. He was more anxious than ever to get out of there.

"Simone, we have to talk," Todd began evenly.

Simone rested her head on his shoulder. "I love these quiet times together, don't you?"

Todd shrugged away from her, putting distance between them. "It's over, Simone. I came here to tell you that I don't want to see you anymore."

Simone's sweet expression vanished and was replaced with a hateful stare. "Just like that?"

Todd nodded. "We've had some fun times, but it would never work between us in the long run. We'll both be happier if we go our separate ways."

"Save the sappy lines for your high-school girls!" Simone retorted. She jumped up and began pacing.

Todd rose to his feet. "Good-bye, Simone."

She whirled around and faced him with a fierce look in her eyes. "Fine, Todd, if that's what you want. But you can kiss your modeling career good-bye."

That stopped him. "What do you mean?" he asked, all of his nerves on alert.

Simone let out a nasty laugh. "I'm going to make you pay for this, Todd," she growled, stabbing the air between them with her carrot. "By the time I'm through with you, the closest thing you'll get to a modeling gig is if you become an escaped felon and they hang your picture up at the post office." With that, Simone stormed out of the room.

Todd's mind was reeling as he left her apartment and got into the elevator. He was glad that his relationship with Simone was finally over. But the notion that he'd just ended his career as well filled him with panic. He slumped against the elevator wall and hung his head. *Without modeling jobs my new independent lifestyle is going to be totally miserable,* he thought.

"I can't believe how much has happened in the past two weeks," Jessica commented to Amy Sutton and Lila Fowler that evening as she floated around her family's backyard pool on an inflatable raft.

Amy was lounging on a patio chair in a blue bikini. "I'm ready to go back to my own life," she said. "But I really enjoyed working with my mom." Dyan Sutton was a sportscaster at WXAB, the local TV network where Amy had served as a production assistant.

Sitting on the edge of the pool in a white maillot, with her feet dangling in the water, Lila sighed wearily. "I'm just glad it's over," she proclaimed. "One more day of that internship, and they would've had to rush me to the hospital for exhaustion."

Jessica rolled her eyes. She knew that to Lila, "exhausting" meant having to answer phones while you were trying to touch up your manicure. Lila hadn't taken the internship program seriously from the start and had settled for a boring position as a receptionist at Fowler Enterprises, her father's computer company.

"My internship turned out great," Jessica said. "Quentin says I have what it takes to be a supermodel."

Lila snorted. "Yeah, right."

Jessica giggled. Besides being her best friend, Lila was also her biggest rival. "When we were at Planet Hollywood last night, he introduced me to some people from the Carlmary modeling agency," Jessica bragged. "And two nights before that I met Eddie Rook."

"Whoopee," Lila drawled, kicking droplets of water on Jessica.

"I also saw Tina Baker at the Edge," Jessica told Lila. "She remembered me from your parents' wedding."

Amy raised her knees and wrapped her arms

around her legs. "What's it like, going out with a guy that old?"

Jessica chuckled at the strange question. "He's in his early twenties," she countered. "I wouldn't call that old. Quentin is sort of a jerk, but he can help me get my career going, and that's what matters." She sighed. "I just wish it hadn't cost me my relationship with Cameron." Jessica closed her eyes as a pang of regret sliced through her heart like a knife. It hurt even to think about him and what might have been. . . .

"The guys at school are *so* boring," Amy complained.

"Most guys are," Lila replied, with a bitter edge in her voice.

"What about the one you met at camp?" Amy asked. "You haven't talked about him for a while."

Jessica shifted onto her side, dipping the float. She realized that Lila hadn't gushed over Bo Creighton, her long-distance boyfriend from Washington, D.C., for some time. "Amy's right," Jessica said. "It's strange not to hear you say 'Bo this' and 'Bo that' every time you open your mouth."

Lila shrugged. "Bo is fine," she said wearily. "I'm just getting tired of dating over the phone."

"Isn't it weird for us to be sitting like this on a Saturday night?" Amy wondered aloud. "I mean, here we are, three of the most popular girls at SVH. . . ."

Jessica slipped off the float and swam to the

edge of the pool. "You're absolutely right," she declared. "In two days we have to go back to school. I say we should hit the beach disco right now and celebrate our last weekend as working women."

Curled up in her chaise longue, in her most comfortable faded jeans and a loose-fitting white sweater, Elizabeth was writing in her journal. Jessica and her two best friends, Lila Fowler and Amy Sutton, were outside in the pool, the faint sounds of their splashing and laughter drifting through the open window. *I wish I could stop thinking about Todd,* Elizabeth wrote. *I guess I am because it's Saturday night. My brain seems to be lagging behind reality because it still can't figure out why I'm not on a date with him tonight. Enid and Maria will be coming over in a while. I think they're trying to keep me from getting too depressed.*

Elizabeth paused, tapping her pen against her chin as she thought. She heard Jessica and her friends running upstairs and into Jessica's room. A moment later rock music blasted through the walls, loud enough to set Elizabeth's teeth on edge. She thought of getting up to complain, but then the volume dropped to a more reasonable setting.

Elizabeth read what she'd written and grimaced. *I'm drowning in self-pity!* she chided herself. Suddenly Jessica, Amy, and Lila burst in through the door of the bathroom that connected the twins' bedrooms, all three of them wrapped in damp towels.

"Where's your tan leather belt?" Jessica asked, already digging through Elizabeth's closet.

Elizabeth sighed wearily. She didn't even have the energy to protest.

"We heard what happened at your internship," Amy said as she towel-dried her blond hair.

Lila sat down on Elizabeth's bed. "I think it's just awful what that woman did to you."

Just then the phone rang. Jessica grabbed the extension on Elizabeth's nightstand. "No, this is her sister, Jessica," she told the person on the other end. "Who may I tell her is calling?"

A wide-eyed look of shock came over Jessica's face. She handed the phone to Elizabeth and whispered, "It's Leona Peirson."

Chapter 8

Elizabeth gulped in a quick breath of sheer panic. Her hands trembled as she took the phone from her sister. "Hello?" she murmured, lowering herself to the edge of her bed. She presumed Leona was calling about the stolen tape recorder.

"I'm sure you didn't expect to hear from me, did you?" Leona asked.

Elizabeth mumbled a vague response.

"We parted on such bad terms. I just can't let things stand as they are between us," Leona explained. "After all, things were terrific at the start. You're a very bright and talented young woman."

Elizabeth wrapped the telephone cord around her finger as she listened incredulously. Jessica, Amy, and Lila were crowded around her with rapt expressions on their faces.

"I want you to know that I have a lot of respect

for your ability," Leona continued. "You really surpassed my expectation of an intern. I know you'll go far in the business world."

"Thanks," Elizabeth muttered dryly. "But what you did was so unfair!"

Leona chuckled. "Elizabeth, you're naive. It happens all the time in the corporate world. Remember what I told you at the very beginning, the day you first showed up at my office?" she asked. "Talent, skill, and hard work are the minimum expectations. Getting ahead takes a whole lot more. And sometimes people get hurt." She paused. "I'm sorry it had to be you."

So am I, Elizabeth added silently.

"But I think you've learned an important lesson—and you can thank me for that," Leona stated evenly.

Elizabeth exhaled sharply. "Gee, *thanks,* Leona," she retorted sarcastically. "I guess having my idea stolen, my proposal plagiarized, getting fired, and being thrown out of the Mode building was all worthwhile."

"OK, we both know 'Free Style' is a fantastic idea," Leona admitted. "But let's be realistic. You don't have the experience and finesse to pull off a project of that scope—yet."

"That still doesn't make it right for you to reject my proposal and then pass it off as your own," Elizabeth argued. Jessica gave her a thumb-up sign. Amy leaned over to whisper into Lila's ear, jostling the bed.

"Try to understand, Elizabeth. This project is

worth much more to me than to you. Its value to you might be what—an A-plus on your report card?" Leona asked snidely. "For me 'Free Style' means more of the two things that make this world go round: power and money."

Elizabeth rolled her eyes, sending Jessica, Amy, and Lila the silent message, *This woman is too much!*

"You're a very intelligent girl," Leona said. "I won't insult you by saying that what I did was right. But I'll make it up to you someday."

"Don't bother," Elizabeth snapped. The doorbell rang at that moment; Jessica gestured for Amy and Lila to answer it.

Leona laughed. "You have a lot of spunk too."

Elizabeth clenched her jaw. Leona's condescending tone made her blood boil.

"We need to put some closure on this whole thing," Leona said. "Let me take you to lunch tomorrow. There's a fabulous little French café in Flora Beach that I'm sure you'd enjoy."

Isn't she gracious! Elizabeth thought sarcastically.

"Is twelve-thirty OK for you?" Leona pressed.

Elizabeth squeezed the corner on her bottom lip between her teeth as she considered the invitation. A heart-to-heart talk with Leona over lunch might be just the perfect solution to her dilemma. *Especially if I get the whole thing on tape!* Elizabeth reasoned.

Amy and Lila returned to the room, followed

by Maria and Enid. "What's going on?" Maria asked in a stage whisper. Jessica hissed at her to be quiet, and everyone sat back down on the bed. Elizabeth shifted sideways as the mattress dipped.

"OK, Leona." Elizabeth cleared her throat. "I'll meet you for lunch tomorrow." Ignoring the collective gasp of surprise from the other girls in the room, she took down the directions to the restaurant.

By the time she hung up the phone, Elizabeth felt incredibly energized. "Hi, guys," she greeted the new arrivals. "I just lined up a power lunch."

"I can't believe you want to go out to lunch with *her*," Lila said, wrinkling her nose.

Elizabeth grinned. "I wouldn't miss it for the world."

"Did she give you a reason why she wanted to see you?" Enid asked.

"Closure," Elizabeth replied. "She says she wants to put closure on this whole ordeal—and I plan to do just that. I'm going to gather enough evidence over lunch to fix her once and for all!"

Beaming, Jessica gave her a hug. "That's my twin!" she said proudly.

Todd turned up the volume on his car radio as he drove toward Sweet Valley on Sunday morning. The traffic on the interstate highway was heavy, probably from people trying to escape the hot, sweaty city for the day. In the rearview mirror Todd could see a gray haze over the L.A. skyline.

He tried to imagine what Elizabeth was doing at that very moment. *Having brunch with her family?* he thought. *Maybe swimming in her pool?* Todd sighed. He recalled Sunday walks on the beach with Elizabeth, her hand in his as they sidestepped the waves. Sometimes they'd drive to Secca Lake for a picnic. . . .

Todd wondered how he could've risked all that he'd had with Elizabeth—for a girl like Simone. Looking back over the past two weeks, he seemed to have made some of his stupidest moves of all time. "What was I *thinking?*" he asked himself aloud.

The drive seemed to take forever, but finally he reached the exit that led to Sweet Valley. Todd suffered a pang of homesickness as the familiar sights of the town came into view. But most of all he was eager to see Elizabeth. He couldn't stand to be apart from her, knowing how badly he'd hurt her.

Heading toward Calico Drive, Todd got caught at every single traffic light, each one raising his frustration level a notch.

Finally! he silently cheered as he turned onto Elizabeth's street. But as he neared the Wakefields' house he saw the twins' Jeep pulling out of the driveway. *Let it be Jessica,* Todd hoped.

He got there just as the Jeep cleared the driveway and took off down the street—with Elizabeth at the wheel. Todd honked his car horn, but she didn't look back.

"Elizabeth!" he hollered uselessly, watching

as the Jeep turned left at the end of the block.

Todd tightened his grip on the steering wheel and followed. He *had* to speak to her. He couldn't put off his apology any longer.

So tell me, Leona . . . have you decided what to call the readers' column? Are you planning to use my *original name for it?* Elizabeth mentally rehearsed as she drove along the coastal highway. *Do you feel the budget projections* Reggie *came up with are realistic?*

Elizabeth chuckled softly. She was surprised to find that she was actually *enjoying* herself. Even the drive was turning out to be pleasant. The day was sunny but not too hot, and although the traffic was heavy, it was moving at a steady pace.

I'm not sure if the blowups of the sample columns I *did were striking enough. If you* had *done them, would you have used a colored border?* Elizabeth imagined herself asking. She was sure her lines would get Leona talking.

Following the directions Leona had given her, Elizabeth got off the highway and turned onto a county road that meandered along the cliffs overlooking the ocean. The sharp, winding turns forced her to drive slowly, but Elizabeth didn't mind because it allowed her to better appreciate the breathtaking scenery.

Elizabeth realized that she wasn't at all nervous about meeting Leona—probably because she was so well prepared. She'd been coached for hours the night before by her friends, her twin, and her twin's friends. Enid and Maria had teamed up against Jessica, Lila, and Amy to argue the best way to entrap a guilty person. The debate had generated lots of great ideas and a complete script of questions and comments to get Leona talking about "Free Style."

Elizabeth touched the small tape recorder in the pocket of her ivory linen blazer and smiled. Her plan was going to be sweet irony—Leona would be caught with her own equipment.

There wasn't much traffic on the county road, but after she'd driven a few miles, Elizabeth became aware of a black pickup truck following close behind her. Assuming its driver wanted to pass, Elizabeth touched her foot to the brake to slow down, hoping to make it easier for the truck to get around the Jeep.

But when she checked the rearview mirror, the truck was still cruising close behind. A blond-haired man with a thick mustache was at the wheel. Elizabeth stuck her left arm out the window, waving for him to pass. *What is he waiting for?* she wondered when he didn't take the hint.

Elizabeth tried to increase the distance between their two vehicles by speeding up a bit, but the other car stayed with her, moving closer until it was right on her tail. She glanced in the rearview mirror and saw that the driver was laughing. "What a creep!" Elizabeth muttered heatedly.

Just then she felt a *thump* from behind. The sudden impact caused her to jerk the steering wheel. The Jeep glided across the center median into the left lane before she could bring it back.

Shaken, Elizabeth pushed down on the gas pedal, desperate to get away from the crazy driver. But like an evil shadow, the truck clung to the back of the Jeep. As they whipped around a sharp curve, tires squealing, he hit her again. The Jeep swerved dangerously close to the edge of the cliff.

Horrified, Elizabeth struggled to maintain control of the Jeep. *Is he trying to run me off the road?* her mind screamed. The answer became obvious as the truck slammed her again.

Elizabeth gripped the steering wheel with both hands and pushed down on the gas pedal. The truck also picked up speed. It shifted to the left lane and pulled up right beside her.

"Hey, gorgeous!" the driver yelled to her. "Blow me a kiss!"

Elizabeth faced forward. She felt beads of sweat dripping down her face as she concentrated on maneuvering along the twisting, narrow road. Suddenly the black pickup sideswiped the Jeep.

"Stop!" Elizabeth screamed, her eyes blurred with hot tears. The driver honked his horn and hit her again.

Elizabeth held her breath as she pushed the gas pedal down all the way. Terrified, she fishtailed around the next sharp curve, her tires screeching.

Before she managed to straighten out the wheel, the crazy truck bumped her again from behind. Elizabeth's heart jumped into her throat as the Jeep swerved close to the edge of the cliff—close enough for her to catch a glimpse of the shimmering blue water far below.

Chapter 9

Where did she go? Todd wondered as he drove along a narrow mountain road in the middle of nowhere. He'd followed Elizabeth out of Sweet Valley but had lost sight of her in the heavy traffic on the interstate. Some time later Todd had caught a glimpse in his side-view mirror of a black Jeep driving off the highway. Hoping it was Elizabeth, he had gotten off at the following exit and backtracked to the ramp that the Jeep had taken.

Now, after driving along the twisting path high above the ocean, Todd wished that he'd stayed on the interstate. He hadn't seen any other vehicles for some time and he had no idea where he was going.

Looks like I made another big mistake, he assumed, reproaching himself. It seemed his only option was to head back to Sweet Valley and wait for Elizabeth at her house. *I'll wait as long as it takes,* he vowed.

Just as he was about to pull over and turn around, he spotted a black Jeep in the distance—and a black pickup truck following on its tail. All of a sudden the truck rammed into the Jeep, sending it fishtailing into the left lane.

A fist of cold panic squeezed Todd's gut. "Elizabeth!" he cried, his foot pushing down heavily on the gas pedal. Todd felt absolutely certain it was her Jeep—and that she was in grave danger.

Todd had no idea why someone was trying to hurt Elizabeth, but he knew he wouldn't let it happen. He whipped around a sharp curve without braking, fishtailing more than ninety degrees before he was able to straighten out the wheels. Pushing his BMW to faster and faster speeds, he raced forward. Within seconds the black truck was just ahead—still riding dangerously close to the Jeep's back bumper.

Todd glanced at the license plate and repeated it silently to himself over and over, committing it to memory. Suddenly the truck lurched forward and bumped into the Jeep.

Horrified, Todd cursed loudly. The Jeep swerved onto the shoulder of the road, then jerked back onto the road too far, veering into the left lane.

Keep it steady, Elizabeth! Todd's mind screamed. He held his breath as she straightened the wheels.

Quickly devising a plan, Todd moved into the

left lane and pulled up alongside the truck. He caught only a brief glimpse of the driver, but in that moment of fear it was as if Todd's brain had snapped an instant photo of the man's short blond hair, flat nose, bushy mustache, and flabby chin.

Todd pushed forward ahead of the truck and slowly began steering his car to the right, his fingers gripping the wheel so hard, they felt numb. The guy was honking his horn crazily, but Todd kept moving over, trying to wedge his way in behind Elizabeth's Jeep, forcing the other driver to slow down.

Elizabeth steered around a hairpin curve, then ventured a glance in her rearview mirror. "Todd!" she screamed. Seized with panic, she pulled over to the narrow shoulder of the road and jumped out of the Jeep. Todd had been right behind her a second ago, with the crazy truck bearing down on *him*.

Elizabeth started running, terrified at what she might find. She imagined Todd's BMW lying in a mangled heap at the bottom of the cliff. . . .

Elizabeth stopped short as she came around the bend in the road. Just a few yards ahead Todd was standing next to his BMW, shading his eyes with his hand. Both he and his car appeared to be in great condition. Farther down the road she spotted the black truck driving away.

Elizabeth uttered a cry of relief and rushed into his arms. They held each other wordlessly for a long moment.

"I've never been so glad to see you in all my life!" Elizabeth said finally, still trembling in the aftermath of her harrowing experience.

Todd continued to hold her tightly. "I'm just glad I got here in time. Oh, Elizabeth, if I had lost you . . ."

She nodded and rested her head on his shoulder, letting his warm strength soothe her frazzled nerves. He smelled of sunshine and spicy aftershave. Elizabeth almost wished she could stay in that very spot forever.

Suddenly her mind shot out a warning, just a name—*Simone*. Tearing herself away, Elizabeth stepped back, her heart squeezing painfully. No matter how much she still loved Todd—or how badly she wanted to stay in his arms—he wasn't hers anymore. *Simone is his girlfriend now,* Elizabeth reminded herself sadly. The fact that he'd just saved her life didn't mean that he wanted to come back to her.

Todd gently pushed a lock of her hair behind her ear. "I was so scared, Elizabeth," he said, his voice thick with emotion, "when I saw that truck hit the Jeep . . ." He drew in a shaky breath. "What was going on anyway?" he asked. "Do you know the guy who was driving?"

Elizabeth shook her head. "Some jerk playing games, I guess."

Todd muttered an oath. "This is a pretty stupid place for that sort of game. It's probably a four-hundred-foot drop to the bottom of the cliff."

"I know." Elizabeth closed her eyes, trying forget the sheer terror she'd felt when the Jeep had nearly skidded to the edge of the cliff.

"How bad did he damage your Jeep?" Todd asked.

Elizabeth shrugged. "I didn't even look. I just jumped out and came running to see if you were all right."

Todd squeezed her hand, then entwined his fingers with hers. "Let's go check it out," he suggested.

Hand in hand, they walked along the side of the road toward the spot where she'd left the Jeep. "I was on my way to meet Leona Peirson for lunch when that black pickup appeared out of nowhere," Elizabeth explained.

Todd's lips twitched. "Figures you'd be on your way to a business lunch on a Sunday afternoon," he gently teased.

A veil of tears blurred her vision. Elizabeth drew in a deep breath and told him everything that had happened at *Flair* between her and Leona over the past week. "But I can't prove any of this," she pointed out. "So I agreed to meet her today for lunch today, hoping she'd let something slip during the conversation—which I planned to record as evidence."

"Sounds like a great idea," Todd said.

When they reached the Jeep, Elizabeth was surprised to discover how little damage there was—nothing more than a few scratches and a small dent on the side. Todd pointed out the flecks of black paint from the other car.

Elizabeth cautiously opened the driver's-side door and peered inside the cab. Her bag had fallen off the seat, its contents strewn across the floor. But other than that, everything seemed perfectly normal.

"Would you like me to drive you to the restaurant?" Todd offered.

Elizabeth shook her head. "Thanks. But I'm too upset to go through with it now."

Todd smiled tenderly. "Then let me take you home. I'll make arrangements to get the Jeep back to Sweet Valley." He moved closer, as if to kiss her. "You're so special to me, Elizabeth," he whispered, his breath softly fanning her face. "I want to take care of you. . . ."

Elizabeth jumped back, even though she desperately wanted to kiss him. "I'll be fine, really," she responded, struggling to keep the ache in her heart from seeping into her voice. "I can get home on my own."

"But I want to help," Todd insisted. "You're still upset. I can tell."

Elizabeth swallowed painfully. "There's nothing more you can do," she said. Although she dreaded having to drive the Jeep all the way back to Sweet Valley, she felt too vulnerable to accept Todd's help. *Maybe Jessica, Enid, or Maria can come and meet me,* she thought hopefully.

"There's no way I'm going to leave you here alone," Todd declared, reaching for her hand.

Elizabeth drew back her hand. "Don't worry

about me," she replied. "My friends and Jessica will provide any help I need."

Desperate to escape before she broke down in tears, Elizabeth slipped behind the wheel, slammed the door shut, and started the engine.

Suddenly her whole body started shaking. She was terrified. She couldn't even make her foot move off the brake.

Todd started walking toward her. *I have to get out of here!* she told herself firmly. She put the Jeep in gear, then bent over the steering wheel, almost hugging it. Cautiously she slid her foot over to the gas pedal.

Todd leaned over the door and peered at her through the window. "Are you sure you're all right?" he asked.

"Never better," Elizabeth lied. Without looking him in the eyes, she shot him a quick, forced smile. Finally he stepped away from the Jeep.

Gulping down her fear, she inched the Jeep away from the shoulder and fumbled through a K-turn.

Elizabeth waved to Todd and drove away, forcing herself not to look back.

Jessica rushed into her house that evening, loaded down with shopping bags. Quentin had called her earlier and had *ordered* her to be ready by seven-thirty for a very important dinner party at Spago's, one of the most famous and elite restaurants in Los Angeles. Jessica had immediately flown into a panic over what to wear. Elizabeth had the Jeep, so Jessica had called Lila to arrange a trip to Valley Mall.

Jessica found two messages on the answering machine. One was from her parents, saying they would be home late that evening. The other was from Elizabeth: "Jessica, the mission was aborted. Call me at Reggie Andrews's."

Jessica frowned, wondering what had happened. But she didn't have time to find out just then. She ran upstairs to her room and dumped her packages on the bed. She'd found two spectacular outfits: a long, pale yellow silk sheath and a short deep green brocade dress with cutaway shoulders and a stand-up collar. She hadn't been able to choose between them, and since she was in such a hurry, she'd bought them both, along with a few accessories. She'd charged everything on her mother's credit card, which was supposed to be for emergencies only. But Jessica figured that looking good at Spago's qualified as an *extreme* emergency.

An hour later Jessica stood in front of her mirror, admiring her reflection. She'd decided on the long dress she'd bought at the Designer Shop. Its pale yellow shade brought out the sun-streaked highlights in her hair. The scooped bodice was adorned with delicate seed pearls sewn in vertical rows. Jessica also thought the body-skimming cut of the skirt showed off her lean curves to their best advantage.

Jessica turned her head slightly, loving the way

her hair moved with its new, stylish cut. *I look like a celebrity fashion model,* Jessica thought optimistically.

Although she knew her height was a mark against her, Jessica believed the dress made her look a bit taller, especially with the strappy high-heeled mules she'd bought at Kiki's.

Jessica pulled the cap off a lipstick tube. Just as she was about to smooth it across her lips, Cameron's words came back to her, hitting her like a bucket of cold water. *Too bad your insides aren't as attractive as your outside,* he'd remarked derisively.

"No!" Jessica snapped, trying to push away the painful memory. She tried to concentrate on her high hopes for the upcoming evening, reminding herself that Quentin would be arriving any minute.

Jessica gave up and tossed the lipstick into her evening bag. Forgetting Cameron was impossible. If he would give her another chance, she'd gladly break up with Quentin. Even if it meant giving up her chance to become the next supermodel of the fashion world. *Nothing is worth losing the guy I love,* Jessica decided.

She only wished she could tell Cameron how she felt. But she had no idea how to get in touch with him. Jessica had tried to find his number, but there wasn't a listing for a "Cameron Smith" in Los Angeles or any of the surrounding towns.

Jessica heard a car pull up in front of the house. She glanced out her bedroom window as the Corvette whipped into the driveway and noisily honked its horn. "How *charming,* Quentin," she grumbled.

She grabbed her bag and rushed downstairs. Although Jessica firmly believed in keeping a guy waiting, it didn't seem like a wise move to try with Quentin. He was enough of a jerk to drive off without her.

The moment Jessica got into his car, Quentin turned to her and asked, "How long were Todd Wilkins and your sister dating before they broke up?"

Jessica fastened the seat belt. "Cute opening line, Quentin," she muttered sarcastically. "But whatever happened to 'Hello, Jessica, you look lovely tonight'?"

"You do," Quentin responded automatically. He backed out of the driveway, then spared her a quick glance. "The dress was a good choice," he added, almost as an afterthought.

"I spent the entire afternoon at the mall and must have tried on at least a hundred different outfits," she said.

"Were they pretty serious?" Quentin asked, drumming his fingers on the steering wheel.

Jessica nodded. "Some of the dresses I found were way too formal looking for me. But I didn't want anything too sporty because—"

"I meant Todd and Elizabeth," Quentin clarified. "Were they serious about each other?"

Jessica glared at him resentfully. "Why do you want to know all this?" she demanded.

"I'm just curious," Quentin replied.

Jessica crossed her arms and exhaled sharply. "They were *too* serious, if you ask me."

Quentin nodded pensively. "I suppose Todd and

Elizabeth have a lot of things in common, huh?"

"Who cares?" Jessica snapped. If Quentin was trying to figure out a way to get back together with Simone, Jessica wasn't about to help him. But despite her efforts to change the subject, Quentin continued quizzing her about Elizabeth and Todd's relationship until they arrived at Spago's.

Jessica's spirits rose as she noticed the paparazzi hanging around the entrance, ready to snap their cameras at any celebrities who might appear. *I'm really here,* she marveled.

"This is a major photo op, so be sure to smile as we walk into the restaurant," Quentin instructed.

Jessica raised her eyebrows. "Oh, so you *do* remember why we came?" she asked pointedly. "I was afraid we would be discussing my sister's love life all night."

"And no sarcasm," Quentin returned dryly.

Jessica smiled brightly, too excited about the great possibilities ahead of her to remain annoyed with Quentin. She felt like a world-class celebrity as they strolled into the restaurant, with paparazzi cameras snapping their picture.

Jessica noticed a hot-looking guy in a dark tuxedo standing just inside the door. Something about him was familiar. . . . *A movie star, maybe?* she wondered. The guy turned slightly, and his gaze met Jessica's. With a start she realized it was Cameron. His gorgeous brown eyes widened, as if he were equally shocked to see her.

Quentin clasped Jessica's elbow firmly, but she shrugged her arm free and rushed over to Cameron. She didn't care if he was only a waiter; Cameron was the guy she loved, and she wanted him to know. "I can't believe it's really you!" Jessica exclaimed, her heart dancing joyfully. "You disappeared from *Flair*, and I had no idea how to get in touch with you."

Cameron rocked back on his heels, his hands deep in the pockets of his dark pants. "Well, here I am," he said dryly.

Jessica smiled brightly, exhaling a shaky sigh. Just standing near him made her feel as if she were riding an emotional roller coaster. Her mouth was dry, and a rapid pulse fluttered in her neck. There was so much she wanted to say, but the absent look in his eyes suddenly made her feel intimidated. "I'm glad you found another job, Cameron. This must be a great place to work," she commented.

Cameron narrowed his eyes. "What do you mean?"

"Don't tell me the hotshot people who eat here are lousy tippers," she said, laughing. "Aren't they afraid you waiters will leak it to the tabloids?" He gave her a strange look, as if he had no idea what she was talking about.

"You *do* work here, don't you?" Jessica asked.

Cameron looked away. "Yeah. Sure, whatever," he mumbled.

Jessica thought she knew the reason for his sullen reaction. "Cameron, I don't think any less of you because you're a waiter," she assured him honestly.

"Thanks," he replied bitingly. "But I'm in sort of a hurry." He turned to go.

Jessica winced at his brusque manner. "Please wait, Cameron."

"Your *date* is glaring at us," he said with a smirk, looking over her shoulder.

Jessica uttered an exasperated sound and signaled to Quentin that she would only be a minute. Then she turned back to Cameron and smiled softly. But there was no encouragement in his eyes.

Determined to make him understand, Jessica pressed on. "I love you, Cameron. Whether you believe me or not, it's true."

Cameron folded his arms and stared at her incredulously. "Those are nice words, Jessica. But it's hard to believe you, considering you're out with Quentin tonight."

"Forget Quentin," Jessica insisted. "I won't ever see him again if that's what you want." *After the swimsuit layout appears in* Flair, *my career will probably take off on its own,* she thought.

Cameron snorted. "Am I supposed to be flattered?"

"I don't care if you are or not," Jessica replied sharply. "But you know as well as I do, Cameron Smith, we belong together. Or are you too scared to admit it?"

Cameron was silent for a long moment. Jessica held her breath, hoping . . .

"Jessica, come on," Quentin called behind her.

She groaned and waved at him over her shoulder.

Cameron raised his eyebrows. "I think your table's ready, Jessica. As for me, my shift is over. See you around."

"Wait!" Jessica begged desperately.

As if he hadn't heard her, Cameron turned around and walked out of the restaurant.

Tears stung in her eyes as she watched him go. *Why won't he believe me?* she thought, her heart writhing in pain.

Chapter 10

"Are you feeling any better, Liz?" Enid asked as she scooped a spoonful of fried rice onto her plate and passed the carton to Maria. They were sitting in Reggie's living room, wearing jeans and sweatshirts, their plates balanced on their laps. Numerous white takeout cartons of Chinese food were lined across the coffee table.

Elizabeth had changed out of the linen suit she'd worn to meet Leona into comfortable jeans and a gray sweatshirt borrowed from Reggie. "I think I'm feeling better," she answered softly. Although she was still very upset, she was no longer trembling uncontrollably. After she'd driven away from Todd that afternoon, Elizabeth had quickly realized she was in no condition to be driving a motor vehicle. She'd pulled into a roadside gas station and called Reggie.

Reggie had insisted on coming to get her. She'd brought Elizabeth back to her apartment, then called Enid and Maria to help get Elizabeth and her Jeep back to Sweet Valley.

"Here, you have to keep up your strength," Reggie said, placing a waxed-paper-wrapped egg roll on Elizabeth's plate.

Elizabeth sighed. "What would I do without you guys?" she wondered aloud.

"Avoid greasy food?" Maria quipped, helping herself to more Szechuan chicken.

Reggie groaned. "I've been moping around, eating nonstop for the past two days," she admitted. "Tomorrow I'm going to put together my résumé . . . and get on with my life." A wistful look came into her eyes. Although Reggie hadn't mentioned Gordon's name, she was obviously crushed about what had happened between them.

"I'm so sorry things turned out so terribly," Elizabeth said. "It's all my fault."

"No, it's not," Enid countered.

Maria nodded. "You did what you thought was best."

"They're right," Reggie agreed. "This is Leona's doing. I've always sensed something off-balance in her." She lifted a neat pile of rice to her mouth with her chopsticks and chewed thoughtfully.

"You mean because she's such a workaholic?" Elizabeth asked.

Reggie narrowed her eyes. "No, more than

that." She tipped her head, her chopsticks poised in midair. "Elizabeth, where were you supposed to meet her for brunch?"

"Someplace called La Café des Crêpes," Elizabeth replied. "Why?"

"I've been there. It's in Flora Beach." A strange expression flickered across Reggie's face. "You were following the directions Leona gave you?"

Elizabeth nodded.

"What are you getting at?" Maria asked.

"I'm not sure," Reggie replied. She hesitated for a moment. "There are much easier ways to get to Flora Beach from Sweet Valley."

Enid gasped. "Do you think *Leona* is behind that stunt on the highway? That she actually planned to have someone drive Elizabeth off the road?"

Elizabeth shook her head. "It's not her style," she argued. "Leona Peirson is a white-collar criminal. I don't think she'd resort to hiring a hit man."

"I wouldn't be too sure of that," Reggie warned. "If Leona sees you as a threat, you could be in a lot of danger."

"What kind of a threat could I possibly be to her?" Elizabeth countered. "She's already fired me. I'm history as far as *Flair* and the entire Mode Corporation are concerned." As she spoke them, the words left a bad taste in Elizabeth's mouth. *Leona is the one who should be history,* she thought.

The girls finished eating and began carrying the

dirty dishes and debris into the kitchen. Elizabeth fumed silently as she rinsed the plates and stacked them in the dishwasher.

Finally something inside her snapped. Elizabeth clenched her fist and brought it down hard on the tiled surface of the kitchen counter. "I'm not ready to quit!" she proclaimed.

"There's a little Kung Pao shrimp left," Enid said, offering her a white carton dripping with brown sauce.

Elizabeth exhaled sharply. "I'm talking about *Leona*," she clarified. "The dishwasher is full, by the way."

"It's over," Reggie said firmly. She squeezed dishwasher detergent into the dispenser on the door and replaced the bottle in the cabinet under the sink. "It's time to move on."

"No, it's not over," Elizabeth argued. "We'll still bust Leona. And as soon as Gordon knows the truth, he'll forgive you."

Maria glared at her. "Are you crazy? Leona Peirson might be the one who tried to get you killed, Elizabeth."

"We don't know that for sure," Elizabeth pointed out.

"Drop it," Reggie advised. She patted Elizabeth's shoulder. "Leona is too dangerous to mess with."

"But we can't just let her get away with what she's done," Elizabeth cried. "It's not fair!"

"Neither would it have been *fair* if that guy managed to push you off a cliff," Maria countered. "I think this is one situation where you can be happy just to be walking away in one piece."

Enid and Reggie nodded solemnly. "It's not worth risking your life," Enid said.

A cold, prickling sensation crawled up Elizabeth's spine. *What if they're right about Leona?* she wondered. *And what if she tries it again?*

Todd arrived at the police station shortly after seven that evening, confident that he'd made the right decision in coming. He'd spent the day agonizing over what had happened to Elizabeth. *Someone tried to kill her!* his mind kept repeating. And that someone had nearly succeeded.

Todd's gut twisted into knots at the idea of Elizabeth getting hurt—or worse. Nothing in his life would ever seem right again. *Without her* . . . Todd shuddered at the cold, gray picture that formed in his mind.

He loved Elizabeth with all his heart. And he had resolved to do whatever he could to help her—even if she wouldn't have anything to do with him.

Todd walked over to the police officer sitting behind a sliding window. "I'd like to report an incident that happened this morning on one of the mountain roads," Todd said, aiming his voice through the small opening at the bottom of the glass pane.

The police officer pushed open the window. "An accident?"

"No, a *crime*," Todd insisted. He reached into the pocket of his jeans and pulled out the scrap of paper on which he'd written down everything he could remember about the black Toyota pickup truck and its driver. "A crazy driver tried to run my girlfriend off the road." Realizing what he'd said, Todd swallowed hard. "I mean, my *friend*," he amended with a pang of sadness.

"Come on in and we'll have someone take your statement," the officer said.

A few minutes later Todd was sitting in an office cubicle, telling a police detective named Shirley Wester what had happened to Elizabeth that morning. "I wrote down everything I remembered," he said, handing her his notes. "It was a black Toyota four-by-four. I wrote the license plate number at the top of the page. I also got a good look at the driver," he added.

Detective Wester nodded thoughtfully as she studied the paper Todd had given her. After a few seconds she rose to her feet. "I'll be right back," she said. "I'm going to run a check on this vehicle."

Todd drummed his fingers on his knee, then walked over to the narrow window behind the officer's desk. The sun had already set, but bright spotlights illuminated the area around the building.

Detective Wester returned and abruptly asked, "You're absolutely sure about this information?"

"Yes, I am," Todd replied.

She perched on the corner of her desk and crossed her arms. "You were pretty upset this afternoon. Maybe you got the license number wrong?"

Todd shook his head. "No, absolutely not. I mean—yes, I was upset. That was *why* I made a point of memorizing everything I could about the other car . . . in case something terrible happened and I ended up being the only witness."

Detective Wester stepped behind the desk and sat down. "And the driver? Could you pick the guy out in a lineup?" she asked.

Todd clenched his jaw. "I know I could."

"Sit down, Todd," Detective Wester said, gesturing toward the chair he'd occupied a moment ago.

Todd saw the grave expression on the woman's face. "What's wrong?" he asked as he sank into the chair.

The detective leaned forward. "The car you described belongs to a well-known thug. We've got a file on him thicker than the L.A. Yellow Pages. He freelances his services. At reasonable rates, I hear."

Todd felt the blood drain out of his face. "You think someone *hired* him to hurt Elizabeth?"

Detective Wester raised her hands in a halting

pose. "It's just a theory. We'll know more after we've questioned the suspect. But if you can identify him in a lineup, my job will be a whole lot easier," she told Todd.

"Don't worry, I will," he declared.

"OK," Detective Wester said, shaking Todd's hand. "Soon as we bring him in, I'll give you a call."

Jessica slumped in the passenger seat of Quentin's Corvette as he drove her home that evening. The glamour of Spago's restaurant had been lost on her—she'd daydreamed about Cameron during the entire dinner. She decided to break things off with Quentin once and for all. She knew she'd never be able to get Cameron back into her life if she didn't.

It's over between us, Quentin, Jessica silently rehearsed. *I appreciate all you've done for me. . . . I think you're incredibly talented. . . . I'm sorry it didn't work out for us. . . .* She wondered what Quentin's reaction would be to her decision. He seemed to be the kind of guy who would cover up his hurt feelings with a show of anger. *But artist types are so unpredictable,* Jessica thought. *I just hope he doesn't break down and cry.*

When Quentin pulled up in front of her house, Jessica inhaled deeply and braced herself for the plunge. "I don't want to keep seeing you," she announced.

Quentin gazed at her with a bemused look in his eyes for several seconds without saying a word. Then he shrugged and replied, "OK."

Jessica glared at him. "That's it?" she demanded. "Just 'OK'?"

"What's the problem?" he asked evenly.

Jessica leaned back against the car door and crossed her arms. "Aren't you the least bit upset?"

"Why should I be?" Quentin smiled and squeezed her hand.

Feeling insulted, Jessica raised her chin defiantly and pushed open the car door.

Quentin chuckled. "Get over it, Jessica. This is another one of those things you'd better get used to if you're serious about making it as a model. In the fashion business people come and go—professionally *and* personally."

"Thanks for the advice," Jessica snapped. She jumped out of the car and slammed the door shut. *What a total jerk!* she thought hotly. Without looking back, she marched up the front walk.

She heard Quentin drive away as she entered the house. "Good riddance!" Jessica muttered. She plunked herself down on the living room couch and breathed a sigh of relief. Then she started laughing. *I don't have a single reason to be mad,* she realized. *Everything turned out perfect!* She'd gotten exactly what she'd wanted from Quentin—a big layout in the upcoming issue of *Flair,* which would mean lots of publicity. *And I don't have to kiss up to the creep anymore*, she reminded herself.

Jessica smiled brightly. Now she was free to pursue Cameron, her real love.

"Thanks for helping me bring the Jeep home," Elizabeth told Enid and Maria later that night as the three of them stood in the Wakefields' driveway. Enid had driven the Jeep back to Sweet Valley for Elizabeth, with Maria following them in her Mercedes.

"Are you going to be OK?" Enid asked.

Elizabeth nodded. "I'm planning on driving to school tomorrow morning."

Maria draped her arm around Elizabeth's shoulders. "Our own Miss Nerves-of-steel," she teased gently.

"I don't know about *that*," Elizabeth replied. "But I'm really anxious to get back to my normal life." She inhaled deeply and sighed. *As normal as my life can be without Todd*, she thought sadly. She wished there were a way for them to get back together, but she didn't feel even a shred of hope. *Todd obviously would rather be with a supermodel.*

Elizabeth's eyes watered, and for a moment she was afraid she was going to start sobbing. It seemed she'd lost so much over the past few weeks. Choking back her tears, she forced herself to smile. "You're the best friends in the whole world," she declared.

Maria pulled them all together for a group hug. "We're not too bad," she agreed wryly.

After they drove away, Elizabeth walked to the front door of the house. The instant she stepped inside, her twin came barreling down the stairs.

"Where have you been?" Jessica demanded.

"At Reggie Andrews's apartment for most of the day," Elizabeth replied. "Didn't you get my message?" She lowered her voice to a whisper. "Are Mom and Dad home?"

Jessica shook her head no. "Good," Elizabeth breathed. "I'm not sure I could face them right now. With any luck, they won't notice the Jeep when they come home." She began trudging up the stairs to her room. "Tomorrow will be soon enough to explain the damage."

"But not for me!" Jessica insisted. She followed Elizabeth to her room and sat down on the edge of the bed. "I want the explanation *now*, Liz! What happened? Did you have brunch with Leona?"

"I never made it to the restaurant," Elizabeth explained. Pacing back and forth across her floor, she recalled the entire harrowing ordeal for her sister.

"How horrible!" Jessica exclaimed.

Elizabeth shuddered. "I nearly drove off the cliff. I don't know what I would've done if Todd hadn't been there."

"Thank goodness for Mr. Boring-as-dry-toast," Jessica said. "But it does seem strange. . . ."

"What do you mean?" Elizabeth asked.

Jessica's eyes narrowed. "Leona knew the route you'd be following this morning. I'll bet she's the one who set up the whole thing."

Elizabeth stopped in her tracks. "That's exactly what Enid, Maria, and Reggie said." Then she waved her hand in the air as if to erase the notion. "I just can't see Leona doing something so drastic."

Jessica shrugged. "Maybe Todd set it up so that he could come out looking like a hero."

Elizabeth glared at her twin. "Now there's a *brilliant* theory," she uttered sarcastically.

"You're right," Jessica replied flippantly. "He's not creative enough to come up with a plan like that." She stretched out on Elizabeth's bed and tucked her hands under her head. "So that leaves only one other suspect—Leona Peirson. She must still see you as a threat. Maybe she's worried that you made copies of all your work."

"No, I'm history as far as Leona is concerned," Elizabeth argued. "Although I *wish* I were a threat to her. You can't believe how much I hate losing to that woman!"

Jessica flipped onto her side, facing Elizabeth. "I think it's time for you to back off and get on with your life, Liz."

"You really think I should let her get away with what she's done?" Elizabeth asked, surprised at her sister's reaction.

"Definitely," Jessica said. "Now that Todd is

gone, you can have so much fun. . . ." She swung her legs over the edge of the mattress and jumped up. "And speaking of fun, my photos for the swimsuit layout will be ready tomorrow. I'm going back to the studio first thing in the morning to check them out. I'm dying to see them!"

"What about school?" Elizabeth asked. "You *do* remember classes start tomorrow?"

Jessica shrugged. "Guess I'll have to skip for the day." She crossed the room and slipped into the connecting bathroom.

"Why don't you wait until after school?" Elizabeth suggested, raising her voice to be heard over the sound of running water.

"Can't," Jessica answered. She opened the door and popped her head back into Elizabeth's room. "I have cheerleading practice after school. I'll have to be back in time for that." With a giggle she ducked back into the bathroom.

Elizabeth shook her head, marveling at her twin's priorities. *But Jessica never lets anything stop her from chasing after her goals,* she admitted to herself.

Elizabeth curled up in her chaise longue and stared absently into space. *Did I give up too easily?* she wondered. Sure, she'd tried hard to get back at Leona—and had failed. But now what? Could she forget all that she'd suffered at *Flair* and just slip back into her normal life at Sweet Valley High?

Elizabeth sighed wearily. If she were half as

bold as Jessica, Leona Peirson wouldn't be getting away with all her dirty dealings. *I would go back to L.A. tomorrow and march right into the Mode building. . . .*

Elizabeth blinked. "That's it!" she cried, bolting to an upright position.

A surge of energy tingled through her body, pushing away her gloomy mood as a plan began to take shape in her mind.

Chapter 11

Elizabeth shrieked as Jessica whipped across two lanes of heavy downtown traffic Monday morning to snag a parking spot in front of the Mode building.

Jessica shot her a sideways glance, then backed the Jeep into the tight space. "I hope you haven't been permanently traumatized by what happened to you yesterday, Liz."

Elizabeth rolled her eyes. "If that didn't do it, your driving certainly will."

Jessica giggled, obviously undaunted by the insult. "This is going to be a fun day," she predicted. "We should skip school together more often."

"Thanks, but I'll pass," Elizabeth muttered dryly.

Jessica dropped her keys into her bag, her eyes glittering with excitement. "I shouldn't be more than an hour. Unless the layout is so fabulous that I can't tear myself away," she added, laughing.

Elizabeth smiled, trying to show enthusiasm for her twin's spectacular achievement. But inside, her heart was pounding like a kettledrum. She hadn't told anyone—not even Jessica—that her real reason for returning to the Mode building was to take one last stab at Leona. She'd made up an excuse about needing one more day to recuperate from her near-fatal brush with the black truck.

Jessica hopped out of the Jeep. "You're going to wait for me here, right?" she asked through the open window.

"Right," Elizabeth lied. "I've got a book to read."

"Sounds exciting," Jessica scoffed. "By the way, you look really great this morning. We even match—sort of. Is that a new outfit?"

"Actually, it's yours."

Jessica chuckled. "No wonder I love it. We should take a drive to Sunset Boulevard later and scope out the guys. Dressed like me, you're sure to find a new boyfriend."

Elizabeth exhaled slowly, waves of sadness crashing over her. She didn't want a new boyfriend. *I want . . . Todd,* she thought. "No thanks, Jess," she replied softly.

"Spoilsport!" Jessica shot back. She flicked her wrist in a jaunty wave and walked away.

Elizabeth waited for her sister to join the throng of people entering the Mode building. *Please let this work!* she hoped fervently.

Elizabeth suspected that her friends and Jessica were right—Leona was dangerous. But caught off guard, she probably wouldn't have anything devious planned. And maybe the surprise of seeing Elizabeth again would help loosen her tongue.

Elizabeth stepped out of the Jeep and locked it. The small tape recorder was in an outside pocket of her canvas bag, ready to pick up any shred of evidence Leona might let drop. *I hope she's in the mood to brag about what she did,* Elizabeth thought.

After having being escorted out by a security guard three days ago, Elizabeth felt nervous about returning to the Mode building. She tried her best not to look guilty as she walked across the lobby. If anyone stopped her, she was prepared to say that she was Jessica. But Elizabeth was relieved when she made it into the elevator without having to lie about her identity.

The ride up to the editorial department seemed to take forever. Elizabeth ignored the cold, measuring stares from the other women in the elevator. A week ago she would have withered under their scrutiny, but now she didn't care a bit if they found her short black skirt and purple tank top lacking in style. She'd selected her outfit carefully that morning, just in case she did have to impersonate Jessica to get into the building.

Elizabeth got off at the eleventh floor. Her legs were shaking, her palms were sweaty, and her heart throbbed as if she'd just run the eleven flights of stairs instead of riding up on the elevator.

For a moment she considered hopping into the next elevator going down.

No way! a strong voice in her head declared. Elizabeth clenched her fists. *I have to do this.* Determined, she headed down the hallway, forcing her legs to walk steadily.

When she reached *Flair*'s editorial department, Elizabeth was relieved to see that the receptionist was busy at the water cooler, her back turned.

Elizabeth quietly snuck past the receptionist's desk and hurried down the corridor toward Leona's office. Then she reached into her canvas bag and turned on the tape recorder. She took a deep breath. "I *can* do it," she whispered.

Holding her head high, Elizabeth burst into Leona's office.

I miss this place already, Jessica realized as she walked around the photography studio, looking for Quentin. The atmosphere seemed to crackle with energy as everyone rushed around amid the jumble of equipment and props.

Jessica finally located Quentin in one of the storage rooms. "Good morning," she said cheerfully.

He glanced at her, then pointed to a stack of boxes on the floor. "Carry this stuff down to my car," he ordered gruffly. "We're doing a shoot on location. You can ride with one of the tech crews or follow in your own car."

"My internship ended on Friday," Jessica informed him.

Quentin eyed her sternly. "So that means you can't carry a few boxes to my car?"

"It means I'm not your flunky anymore," Jessica replied. "I only came to see the swimsuit layout before it goes to print."

"On my desk," he grumbled. "At least make yourself useful and deliver them to the mail room. The issue is being printed tomorrow, and the photographs have to be messengered right away."

Jessica grinned. "I'd be delighted to help you out, Quentin."

"Great," he muttered. "And hurry up."

Thrilled, Jessica scurried over to Quentin's office and found the mailer containing the photos. "My ticket to the top," she murmured excitedly. She grabbed the package and rushed out of the studio.

As she headed for the elevator Jessica carefully pulled out the photographs. She took one look and stopped in her tracks. "*Simone?*" she hissed.

Jessica made a low, growling sound deep in her throat as she shuffled through the rest of the photos. She couldn't believe what she was seeing. The wicked witch appeared in every single shot.

Flames of hot anger blazed through Jessica. "He switched them!" she shrieked.

"Thanks for coming in this morning," a gray-haired police officer said as he ushered Todd into a darkened room. A glass panel spanned the length of one of the walls. Todd didn't have to be told that it was a one-way mirror.

He hadn't expected to be called back to the police station so soon, but he was relieved that the case was getting immediate attention. Todd knew he wouldn't be able to rest easy until they found the jerk who'd tried to hurt Elizabeth.

The officer gestured toward the straight-back chairs facing the one-way mirror. "Have a seat. Soon as you're ready, we'll begin. By the way, I'm Officer Troper," he added.

Todd sat down and mentally prepared himself for the lineup by picturing the driver of the black truck, trying to remember as many details as he could.

A few minutes later eight men filed in on the other side of the glass. "That's him!" Todd declared, immediately recognizing the guy's broad nose and fleshy chin. "Second from the right."

"Take your time, son," Officer Troper advised. "Look at them closely. Study their profiles." Over a telephone intercom he instructed the men to turn from side to side.

"I'm sure," Todd insisted, his hands clenched into fists. He wanted to strangle the creep.

The police allowed Todd to watch the suspect being questioned. Two detectives took turns asking the guy about his whereabouts the previous day. His lawyer, who was sitting next to him in the interrogation room, kept interrupting with objections.

At first the guy denied all the accusations against him. "I didn't even *see* a black Jeep yesterday," he claimed.

What a filthy liar! Todd thought, fuming. Sitting next to him in the observation room, Officer Troper snorted, obviously sharing Todd's opinion of the guy's statement.

Detective Wester slammed her notebook on the table and glared at the suspect. "We have an eyewitness who identified you," she countered in a threatening tone. "A *reliable* witness, who places you at the scene and who even remembered your license plate number. So let's drop the fairy tales right now before I lose my patience."

Todd heard Officer Troper mutter under his breath, "Go, Shirley."

As the interrogation continued, the guy's answers began to sound more and more shaky. His hotshot attitude disappeared, and he seemed to crumple in his seat.

Finally, with a nod from his lawyer, he gave up. "OK, I was there yesterday!" he shouted. "I bumped the Jeep, sideswiped it . . . but I'm not the real criminal. I only did it because I needed the money."

"You're saying someone *hired* you to go after that girl?" Detective Wester asked.

The guy nodded. "Yeah. It was supposed to look like a car accident."

Todd inhaled sharply. *If I hadn't gotten to Elizabeth's house in time to follow her, this creep would have killed her—and walked away free!* he thought hotly.

"Who hired you?" the detective asked the guy.

"First let's discuss the charges against my client," his lawyer interjected. "I think it would be appropriate to discuss a plea bargain in exchange for that information."

"Forget it," Detective Wester replied smoothly. "I can lock up your client right now, just on the basis of his outstanding traffic tickets—and you know it." She glared at the suspect. "Besides, the person who hired him might be someone out of his own imagination."

The guy raised his chin defiantly. "I'm telling you the truth now," he said. "It was a lady named Leona Peirson!" He went on to reveal the details of their deal.

Todd's blood turned to ice as he listened. *Leona Peirson wants Elizabeth dead.* The realization shot his panic level to new heights.

Next to him Officer Troper chuckled derisively. "These lowlifers will say anything to save their hides."

"I believe him," Todd said. He explained what had happened between Leona and Elizabeth over the past two weeks.

The officer picked up the phone and buzzed the extension inside the interrogation room. "The story checks out," he said. "Let's bring the woman in."

A flurry of activity erupted as several more police officers entered the observation room, followed by Detective Wester. "Thanks for your help, Todd," she said, dismissing him. She picked up the phone and gave the order for a police cruiser to be dispatched to the Mode building.

"What about Elizabeth?" he demanded. "She could still be in danger."

"You said she was back at school today, right?" Officer Troper asked.

Todd nodded. "Yeah, but Leona Peirson might have hired someone else to go after her in Sweet Valley."

Detective Wester placed her hand on his shoulder. "Don't worry, Todd. A school building away from the city is probably the safest place your friend could be right now," she told him. "As long as she isn't in L.A., I'm sure Elizabeth is fine."

As Todd drove away from the police station he impulsively decided to go to the Mode building. He wanted to be absolutely sure the police arrested Leona Peirson—so that he could tell Elizabeth she was safe again. It was the least he could do after the terrible way he'd treated her.

Leona appeared startled to see Elizabeth, but she quickly regained her composure. "I'm sorry," she said, folding her arms on her desk. "If you're looking for a job, we don't have any openings."

Seeing the smug expression on her former boss's face, Elizabeth's blood began to simmer, bolstering her courage. "I'm not here for a job," she retorted.

Leona raised her eyebrows. "You just happened to be in the neighborhood?"

Elizabeth slammed the door shut and leaned back against it. "I just want to get one thing straight between us, Leona. I want to hear you admit that it was *my* idea."

Leona smiled innocently. "What idea is that?"

"You know perfectly well," Elizabeth shot back.

"You poor, misguided kid," Leona drawled. "But in spite of what you did to me, I still believe there's hope for you, Elizabeth. You were one of the brightest interns we've ever had here at *Flair.*"

"Just admit it, Leona!" Elizabeth demanded tersely.

Leona grinned. "I'd be happy to discuss whatever you want to know"—she held out her hand—"as soon as you give back my tape recorder."

Elizabeth's jaw dropped.

Leona tipped back her head and laughed. "Did you really think you could get away with stealing it? I didn't get where I am by being stupid."

Elizabeth felt utterly defeated. She'd completely run out of ideas on how to prove her innocence. It seemed Leona had won after all.

"I want it back immediately," Leona said sharply. "Consider yourself lucky that I haven't had you arrested for trespassing and burglary."

Elizabeth slowly dragged herself forward. She placed the tape recorder on Leona's desk, then turned to go.

"Not so fast," Leona said. "We still haven't discussed what's on your mind."

Elizabeth stopped. The heaviness in her chest felt like a granite boulder. She sighed wearily and turned around, then froze in numb terror as she stared at the gun in Leona's hand.

"Sit down, Elizabeth," Leona ordered. "We're going to have a little talk. And when we're finished, you and I will take an early lunch together—someplace nice and secluded. . . ."

Elizabeth nodded automatically, her whole body in a state of shock. But a corner of her mind remained calm and acutely aware of what was going on while calculating and groping for a way out of the situation. A few hazy ideas popped into her head. . . .

"I said sit!" Leona raged.

Elizabeth winced as if she'd been slapped. Then, as she obeyed, she faked a stumble and landed with her arms stretched across Leona's desk. In the span of a heartbeat she reached out and secretly pushed a button on the phone.

"Were you always this clumsy?" Leona chided.

Elizabeth's pulse hammered fiercely as she lowered herself into the chair. "Sorry," she murmured. "I'm *scared*, that's all."

Leona appeared calm, even friendly. "I came back to town Friday morning and called the office," she explained. "As soon as I heard you'd already left for 'the meeting,' I knew exactly what was going on."

She shook her head woefully. "You were out of your league, Elizabeth. Granted, your idea for 'Free Style' was great—but it takes more than ideas to get ahead. You should never have tried to compete with me."

Elizabeth clutched the sides of the chair, her heart in her throat. "OK, fine, you win," she conceded in a thin, shaky voice. "You've gotten away with stealing my idea. Why don't you just let me go now?"

Leona shrugged. "There's nothing I'd like better. But unfortunately your little trick with Gordon Lewis brought the mess to a new level."

An uneasy sensation crawled up Elizabeth's spine. "What do you mean?" she asked.

"The trouble you've caused!" Leona rolled her eyes. "It's as if you'd swung a baseball bat at a wasps' nest. Gordon is completely bent out of shape. He's taking this whole thing much too personally, in my opinion. He's been running around here like a scorned man, ranting and raving. . . . He wants to prosecute Reggie for conspiracy."

Elizabeth gasped. "That's not fair!"

Leona sneered at her. "There you go again, you silly fool," she replied bitingly. "Fair doesn't mean a thing in the real world. Reggie Andrews knew that when she plotted against me. As for you— Gordon wants to make an example out of you for future interns." Leona exhaled with a forced sigh. "I tried to argue on your behalf, but the man is adamant. I'm supposed to be building a case against you . . . pressing charges . . . taking action to seek punitive damages. . . . Like I said, it's a real mess."

Elizabeth was stunned as she tried to make sense of what she was hearing. *Leona stole, lied, plagiarized my work—and now she's holding me at gunpoint. . . . But Reggie and I are the ones being prosecuted!*

"Gordon called me ten minutes ago and ordered me to contact your school and your parents today." Leona leaned forward and grinned. "But you and I know that would be a big mistake."

Elizabeth nodded mutely, her heart in her throat.

"I checked out your background," Leona continued. "How am I supposed to bring down a model student who also happens to be a hotshot lawyer's kid? But I hate loose ends, and since the jerk I hired for the job was a miserable failure . . ."

A cold fist squeezed Elizabeth's heart. "What do you mean?" she asked, fearing the answer.

Leona flashed her a crooked smile and winked. "I missed you at brunch yesterday. Those mountain roads can be treacherous, huh?"

"So it *was* you!" Elizabeth gasped. "You actually want me *dead*?"

"My career is everything to me," Leona stated with a nasty grin. "With Gordon pushing me against the wall, I don't have many options left."

Elizabeth stared at her, wondering how she could have ever admired such a cold-hearted monster. She realized that there always had been a hardness about Leona, a predatory gleam in her brown eyes. Reggie had warned her. But Elizabeth had been blinded to all that by her own ambition.

"It's time for us to go for our drive," Leona announced. She tossed a lock of her dark blond hair behind her shoulder and pointed the gun at Elizabeth's face. "Now move it!" Leona barked.

Chapter 12

Still holding the gun, Leona tucked her crutches under her arms and limped around the desk. A terrible look of violence sparkled in her eyes.

Elizabeth felt paralyzed with fear. A scream clawed in her throat.

"Let's go, *child prodigy*," Leona hissed, striking Elizabeth's leg with one of the crutches.

"No, please!" Elizabeth begged, tears spilling down her cheeks. "I promise not to cause you any more trouble."

Leona sneered and pushed the barrel of the gun against Elizabeth's neck. "It's too late for promises," she growled.

"It *isn't*," Elizabeth pleaded desperately. "I'll tell everyone that I'm guilty, that I tried to pass off your work as my own."

All of a sudden, two police officers burst into

the room. At that very instant Leona pressed the gun into Elizabeth's hands and sagged against her desk.

"Nobody move!" one of the policemen ordered.

Wearing an expression of relief, Leona turned to the officers. "Thank goodness you're here!" she uttered breathlessly, as if *she* were the one who was being threatened at gunpoint.

"Give yourself up," she told Elizabeth. "I know you really didn't mean to hurt me. You're just a mixed-up kid who needs help."

Elizabeth was stunned. Leona's act was absolutely flawless. She actually had tears in her eyes. But the police apparently weren't fooled. One of them approached her with a pair of handcuffs.

"What are you doing?" she asked tremulously. "*I'm* on crutches."

The other officer rolled the chair out from behind Leona's desk and gruffly ordered her to sit down.

"Leona Peirson, you're under arrest for the conspiracy to commit murder," the first policeman stated as they pulled her arms behind the back of the chair and fastened the handcuffs on her wrists. "You have the right to remain silent. . . ."

"You're making a big mistake!" Leona screamed. "You don't have a shred of evidence against me."

The police officer finished reading Leona her rights, then said, "Your scummy friend sang like a canary this morning."

"I don't know what you're talking about," Leona insisted.

The cop shrugged. "He seems to know about you. Says you hired him to do a nasty piece of work yesterday morning."

Leona's nostrils flared. "Obviously the guy is lying."

Gordon Lewis showed up at the door. "Tell them they're wrong," Leona pleaded with him. "They're accusing me without any proof."

"They're not," he replied evenly. "We have all the proof we need, thanks to your conversation with Miss Wakefield."

"And you believe her over me?" Leona retorted. "I don't know why you're turning on me like this, Gordon. You know that Elizabeth Wakefield is a vindictive liar."

Gordon's expression hardened. "Drop the innocent act, Leona. I'm talking about the conversation that took place in this office within the last ten minutes. Your intercom was on the whole time. The receptionist heard everything and called me."

"But how—" Leona turned to Elizabeth, her eyes blazing. "It was *you*, wasn't it? You turned it on!"

Elizabeth grinned. During one of her meetings with Leona, Elizabeth had used the intercom to tell Todd that she didn't want to speak to him ever again. "Guilty as charged," she responded.

Leona cursed everyone—especially Elizabeth—as the police took her away, chair and all.

After she was gone, Gordon turned to Elizabeth. "I owe you an apology," he said. "I'm so sorry for everything you've been put through because of your internship with us. I'd like to make it up to you if I can."

"I'm just glad the nightmare is over," she replied shakily.

"Leona was right about one thing—you are the best intern we've ever had." He reached out and shook Elizabeth's hand. "Anytime you want a job, you've got one," he said.

Elizabeth smiled. "I hope the same goes for Reggie Andrews."

"It certainly does," he said. "I'm going to call her right now and beg her to come back."

As they walked out of the office Elizabeth caught a glimpse of Todd slipping around the corner in the hallway. "What's he doing here?" she wondered aloud.

"You mean Todd Wilkins?" Gordon asked. "He's the one who led the police to Leona."

Elizabeth felt a surge of happiness—and hope. *Maybe Todd really does care about me after all,* she thought.

Jessica stormed back into the studio and confronted Quentin. "What's the meaning of this?" she demanded, waving the photos under his arrogant nose.

"Haven't you got those out yet?" he

complained. "I thought I told you to hurry."

"And I thought this was supposed to be *my* layout," she spat back at him.

Quentin crossed his arms and glared at her. "I'm the one who makes the final decisions around here," he reminded her pointedly.

"But it was settled," she argued. "You said the shots you took of me were fantastic."

"I changed my mind," he replied flippantly, as if it weren't a big deal that Jessica's hopes had been shattered. "Now, if you'll excuse me . . . I've got work to do." He began barking orders to the lighting crew.

Jessica's temper flared. "That's *it*, Quentin? You suddenly changed your mind?" she raged.

Quentin shrugged. "That's right. It's my job to choose the right model. And I decided Simone was better for the job after all." He reached out and gently squeezed her shoulder. "Thanks for stopping by, Jessica. It was nice to see you again. But we're running on an extra-tight schedule this morning, so if you don't mind . . ."

Jessica felt as if she were ready to explode with anger. "You're the biggest jerk I've ever met!"

"I've heard that line before," he quipped. He yelled at one of the technicians, then turned back to Jessica. "Listen, before you go, would you mind checking over the equipment list? We're really shorthanded today."

"I already *told* you, I'm not your flunky anymore," Jessica retorted hotly. "And I'm not leaving until we've settled our business. You promised me a layout in *Flair*, Quentin."

"It didn't work out," he said. "Deals fall through every day in this business."

Just then Jessica heard a familiar voice laughing behind her. Her anger blazed hotter.

Simone walked passed her and slipped her arm around Quentin's waist. "Jessica, you poor little thing," she drawled, pushing out her huge, silicone-filled lips. "Quentin never had any intention of putting you in *Flair*. He was just using you."

Jessica glared at Quentin. "Tell me she's lying."

Quentin ducked his head sheepishly and said nothing.

"You'd better start explaining," Jessica demanded fiercely.

"It was no big deal," he responded defensively. "Simone tried to make me jealous by fooling around with Todd. So I decided to give her a taste of her own medicine."

Jessica was speechless, her jaw hanging as she stared at the pair of them. *And I thought I was doing the using.*

Simone playfully elbowed Quentin in the ribs. "He's such a beast!" she chirped.

Quentin tweaked her nose.

They're a perfectly disgusting match, Jessica realized. *And if I don't get away from them immediately, I'm going to puke.*

◦　　　◦　　　◦

Wanted: swimming pool attendant for upscale fitness club . . . minimum wage w/ weekend bonus. Apply in person: Hollywood Bod. Todd reread the ad and circled it. "Sounds interesting," he murmured.

Todd was sitting at his kitchen table Saturday afternoon, scanning the *L.A. Times* classified section as he ate his lunch of cornflakes and milk—his fourth bowl that day. If he didn't find a job soon, he knew he'd be living on cornflakes for a long, long time.

The past week had been dismal. The only bright spot had been Leona Peirson's arrest. Elizabeth was safe now. *I miss her so much!* Todd admitted to himself. He was aching to see her again. But until he got his life on track, he figured Elizabeth was better off without him.

Lack of money seemed to be the major factor holding him back. When Todd had phoned the photography studio at Mode to get his modeling schedule for the week, he'd been told that there were no sessions planned for him in the near future.

He'd tried contacting Quentin Berg several times since, but the photographer hadn't returned any of his calls. Finally Todd had tried setting up appointments with every modeling agency in the phone book, but no one seemed interested in helping him.

Todd suspected Simone had made good on her

threat to ruin his chances as a model. As much as it angered him, he was still glad he'd broken up with her. He'd walked out on his parents because they'd tried to control him. He wasn't about to put up with a vindictive, controlling girlfriend who was only using him anyway. He wished he'd seen her true nature at the very beginning. If he had, he would still be with Elizabeth.

Todd shook away the sad thought. At that moment his biggest concern was restocking his food supply and coming up with next month's rent. His savings were running out much faster than he'd planned. And since he could no longer count on modeling, it seemed he'd have to work a lot harder than he'd imagined in order to survive on his own.

Todd had planned to continue his education with the help of a private tutor, but that plan was out of the question now. He could barely afford milk to go with the cornflakes, so he certainly couldn't hire a tutor. His choices were to transfer to a Los Angeles public high school, where he wouldn't know a single person, or to drop out of school altogether. He wasn't happy with either option.

Todd scooped up another spoonful of cereal, chewing as he read. *Lawn maintenance assistant, Morgan Retirement Home* . . . He nodded. "An outdoor job," he murmured. "That could be fun."

Someone turned on the television next door and a commercial jingle blasted through the walls, startling him. He clenched his fist and pounded on the wall. His neighbor answered by shouting a string of colorful curses.

Todd rolled up the newspaper and threw it against the wall. *I didn't move to L.A. to live in a dump like this,* he thought, fuming. A cloud of despair swept over him as he considered the hopelessness of his situation. Even with *two* low-paying jobs he wouldn't be able to afford a nicer apartment.

"Stop it!" Todd ordered himself. "I *am* going to make it!" He was determined to show his parents that he could take care of himself—even without them hovering over him day and night, forcing him to obey their rules and curfews.

Todd picked the newspaper up off the floor and carried it back to the table. He spread it open and found his place. *Waiter . . . downtown luncheonette . . .* As he continued reading he heard a crunching noise next to him.

He looked up and saw a fat gray mouse perched on the rim of his cereal bowl.

"What the—," Todd shrieked, jumping up so abruptly that his chair toppled over backward. The mouse glared at him, as if he thought Todd was being terribly rude. Then he boldly reached down and clasped a cornflake between his paws. His cheeks puffed out as he nibbled his prize.

Todd grabbed a pot cover from the cupboard and stalked back to the table. "You've gone way too far this time, and you're going to be sorry," he warned.

Apparently dismissing the threat, the mouse continued munching. Todd wasn't surprised. The creature had been taunting him for days. It was obviously very brave, considering that it had no problem coming right up and challenging Todd to his face.

Todd stalked over to the table. Just as he brought down his makeshift trap the mouse scurried away.

Todd shouted a curse and jerked back his arm, accidentally knocking his cereal off the table. The plastic bowl bounced. Streams of milk and globs of mushy cornflakes shot across the floor.

And right in the middle of the mess the mouse resumed his meal.

"Stay right where you are, you fat ugly thing," Todd growled as he picked up the pot cover again. As he lunged across the floor he nicked his elbow on a piece of chipped linoleum. The mouse darted past him and slipped into a crack under the bottom cabinet.

"You can't run from me forever!" Todd yelled as he wiped drops of blood off his elbow. He'd been trying to corner that mouse for days. Sharing the apartment with it was bad enough. But eating together from the same bowl went way beyond gross. Todd had been pushed to his limit.

"I'm going to get that dirty stinker!" he vowed as he crawled nearer to the spot where the mouse had disappeared. "This is *war*. Man against beast!"

Suddenly he saw the mouse scurry out from

under the cupboard. Todd lunged again, with his bare hands this time, and managed to grab the creature by its tail.

"You're outta here!" he exclaimed victoriously.

Holding the dangling mouse at arm's length, Todd speed-walked out of the apartment and down the four flights of stairs to the front door. "And don't come back!" he grumbled as he set the mouse down on the ground.

Todd brushed his hands and was about to go inside when he happened to catch a glimpse of a man crossing the street toward him. Then he saw who it was, and his whole body stiffened. Mr. Wilkins hesitated at the sidewalk and stared back at Todd.

Not now! Todd moaned to himself. His kitchen was splattered with soggy cereal, and the employment section of the newspaper was scattered across the table. There wasn't any food left in the refrigerator. Todd's father would know immediately how bad things had turned out for him.

Todd stood his ground, his hands in the back pockets of his jeans as he waited. Suddenly Bert Wilkins began waving a white flag. Then Todd saw the moving van parked across the street.

Todd exhaled a long breath, his body nearly sagging with relief. He walked to meet his father halfway. Communicating without words, they exchanged a hug.

"Let's go get your things," Mr. Wilkins said simply.

Todd grinned. "Gladly."

When the last of his stuff was packed into the van, Todd felt better than he had in a long time. He'd finally gotten his life back in order . . . *almost*.

There was just one piece missing. Todd still had to fix the most important thing in his life—his relationship with Elizabeth.

Feeling miserable, Jessica was spending her Saturday curled up in front of the TV, channel surfing as she ate her way through a bag of nacho-cheese-flavored tortilla chips. She couldn't stop thinking of Cameron and of how badly she'd messed up their relationship. *I should have followed him when he walked away from me at Spago's last week. . . . Maybe he would have listened to me. . . .*

Elizabeth walked in, scowling with disapproval. "Jessica, it's two o'clock in the afternoon," she said in an irritating, bossy big-sister tone. "Don't you think you should at least get dressed?"

"I am," Jessica replied tersely.

Elizabeth exhaled sharply. "Oh, yes. White bathrobes are so very *in*," she drawled sarcastically. "I love the accessories too. Those fuzzy pink slippers are this season's fashion *essentials*."

Ignoring her, Jessica flipped to a different station and settled in to watch an infomercial about acne cream.

"Are you sure you don't want to come to the

Plaza Theatre with Enid, Maria, and me?" Elizabeth asked. "They're showing a double feature—two Bette Davis movies for the price of one."

Jessica grimaced. "Have fun."

"We could do something else if you want," Elizabeth offered. Jessica pressed the mute button on the remote control. "Liz, I know you're trying to be helpful, but you're really annoying me."

Elizabeth threw up her hands. "OK, fine—I'm leaving," she said as she backed out of the room.

Jessica turned the volume back up on the TV and changed the channel again.

"Good-bye, Jess," Elizabeth called out to her a few minutes later. Jessica heard the front door open and close, then the sound of the Jeep pulling out of the driveway.

"Alone at last." She sighed wearily. Her parents were also out for the day. Jessica reached into the bag for another tortilla chip.

Jessica had tried phoning Cameron at Spago's, but they'd told her they didn't have anyone named Cameron Smith on staff. She was convinced that it was a lie. After all, she had seen Cameron there with her own eyes.

Maybe Cameron told them to say it because he didn't want to talk to me, she thought sadly. *What if he never calls me?* Returning to school had been terrible. It emphasized the fact that her internship was completely over—and her experience at *Flair* had ended. But Jessica wasn't ready to put it all behind her and start over at SVH.

A tear rolled down Jessica's cheek. She wiped it with the back of her hand and sniffed loudly. "It's all my fault," she muttered. She'd spent her days at school that week in a daze, cursing herself for going out with Quentin when Cameron was the guy she loved.

Knowing that Quentin had been using her made her even more upset. All the time she'd spent putting up with his rude, arrogant behavior hadn't help her career a bit. Jessica remembered how excited she'd been when Quentin had photographed her for what she'd *believed* would be a dazzling swimsuit layout in *Flair.* But it had turned out to be nothing more than a cruel joke.

Jessica mentally kicked herself. *How could I have been so blind?*

The doorbell rang, interrupting Jessica's self-re-crimination. "Go away!" she grumbled. It rang again.

"Can't a girl have a few minutes of privacy in her own home anymore?" she muttered as she dragged herself off the couch.

When she opened the front door, she was surprised to find a deliveryman standing there with an express package addressed to "Miss Jessica Wakefield."

Jessica eagerly signed for the package, her spirits somewhat lifted. She carried it into the living room and set it on the marble coffee table. But when she opened it, her heart sank. In it were the blue pages for the next issue of *Flair,* the one Jessica had *thought* she'd be in.

Her temper flared. *Someone sent this just to torture me!* she presumed. *Is this Simone's sick idea of a joke?*

Sobbing, Jessica threw the pages across the room. "I never want to see a copy of *Flair* magazine again as long as I live!" she raged. "And as for this box of *garbage* . . ."

She decided she would take the nasty little "surprise" out back and burn it. But as she bent down to pick up the blue pages, one of the photographs snagged her attention. Jessica looked closer . . . and saw *herself.* "It can't be," she murmured.

She sat down in the middle of the floor and studied the photo of herself wearing a belted maillot with a sheer cape billowing from her shoulders. The camera had caught her laughing, with her arms gracefully poised at her sides and her windblown hair framing her face.

"This is incredible," Jessica breathed. There was a ten-page spread of *her* looking absolutely gorgeous. She gazed at each photo, mesmerized.

I doubt Simone sent these, Jessica thought, giggling. Curious to know who did, she examined the package. She found a pale gray envelope tucked inside the box, with her name handwritten on the front, and quickly tore it open. It was a formal invitation to a dinner party at the home of someone named Mr. Edward McGee.

Jessica sat down on the couch, her gaze fixed on the embossed card. *Edward McGee,* she mentally repeated. The name was familiar. . . . She racked her brain, trying to remember where she'd heard it.

Suddenly the answer popped into her head. *"E. McGee!"* she exclaimed. "The man who owns *Flair* and the entire Mode Corporation! He wants *me* to eat dinner at his house?"

Jessica's hands trembled with excitement as she checked the date and time on the invitation. "Oh, my gosh, it's for *today!*" she cried. There was a note on the bottom of the card, saying that a limo would be arriving to pick her up at her home at seven P.M.

Jessica looked up at the wall clock and shrieked. "That means I have less than five hours to get ready!" She dropped the card and raced to her room.

Chapter 13

Jessica felt like a princess as she rode to L.A. in the back of a luxurious stretch white limo. She didn't know why Edward McGee had invited her to dinner, but she was positive something wonderful was about to happen.

She was certainly prepared for it, thanks to her recent trip to the Valley Mall. Smoothing the hem of her short, deep green brocade dress, Jessica congratulated herself on her foresight. Stocking up on fabulous outfits had proved to be a stroke of genius.

Jessica gazed out the window as the limo passed through the open gates at the entrance of a very long, winding driveway. Rows of tiny white lights illuminated it on both sides, creating the illusion of a silver-edged ribbon stretched across the sloping grounds.

At the end of the driveway the limo pulled up

in front of a huge Beverly Hills mansion. Jessica could hardly contain her excitement. *I'm going to a party at E. McGee's,* she happily chanted to herself. The driver stepped out of the car and opened the door for Jessica.

A uniformed butler greeted her at the entrance to the mansion with a stiff, formal bow. "Follow me, miss," he said with an equally stiff and formal English accent. He led her into an elaborate study, where a white-haired man was sitting behind a mahogany desk.

The elderly man rose to his feet. With a respectful bow the butler left the room, closing the doors behind him.

Jessica felt somewhat intimidated at first. Then the man smiled warmly, instantly putting her at ease. "Welcome to my home, Miss Wakefield," he said, coming forward to shake her hand. "I'm Edward McGee."

"Thank you, sir," she responded.

He gestured toward a leather chair across from his desk. "Please make yourself comfortable. The other guests won't be arriving for at least another half hour. I wanted an opportunity to meet with you privately."

Jessica couldn't imagine why. She sat down, burning with curiosity.

Mr. McGee returned to his seat behind his desk. "The blue pages of the new issue of *Flair* were sent to you," he said. "I trust you've received them?"

"Yes, I did," Jessica answered brightly.

"I'd like to congratulate you on the excellent job you did modeling. It's always gratifying to discover and develop new talent. That's a goal of all my companies."

Jessica felt a warm glow in response to his compliment. "Thank you," she replied sincerely. She didn't see the need to mention that she hadn't been the first-choice model for the layout or that she'd been "discovered and developed" because of her own conniving and the fact that Simone had thrown one of her nasty temper tantrums the day of the shoot.

"You're a very talented young woman," Mr. McGee remarked.

Jessica smiled. But as much as she was enjoying the conversation, her mind remained puzzled. "Is that why you invited me here tonight?" she asked bluntly.

Mr. McGee chuckled, apparently pleased with her direct question. "Partly," he answered. "But the main reason is that I wanted to introduce you to my son."

A blind date? Jessica groaned to herself. *All this—just to get fixed up with some geeky rich kid?*

"My son has been looking forward to this evening for some time," Mr. McGee was saying. "He's quite a fan of yours, Jessica. And now that I've met you, I can understand why."

Jessica tried to keep her outward expression

187

neutral, but inside she cringed. *Great. I get to spend the evening listening to a spoiled jerk bragging about daddy's millions,* she thought bitterly.

There'd been a time when she might have been impressed by a guy's wealth, but Jessica had learned from recent experience that no amount of money or power could make up for a no-spark romance. Although she didn't want to offend Mr. McGee, Jessica had no intention of going along with his plan. She wasn't about to repeat the same mistake she'd made with Quentin.

"I'm really flattered, Mr. McGee," she began hesitantly. "But you see—"

"I'll be right back," he said, cutting off the rest of her sentence. Before she could say another word, he slipped out of the room.

Jessica clenched her jaw, fuming. "I'm stuck!"

She stood up and began pacing across the room. *As soon as that man comes back I'm going to tell him flat out that I'm not interested in meeting his son,* she promised herself.

Moments later she heard the door open behind her. Thinking it was Mr. McGee, Jessica whirled around, prepared to deliver her speech. But to her amazement, Cameron Smith walked into the room.

Jessica gasped. "What are you doing here?" she asked as she looked around nervously. "You'd better leave!"

Cameron gave her a crooked smile. "Aren't you happy to see me, Jessica?"

"Thrilled," she responded. "But you're going to be in big trouble if you don't get out of here. Mr. McGee will be right back, and if he finds that a former mail-room clerk has crashed his dinner party, he'll have you thrown out for sure—and probably arrested too."

Cameron nodded pensively. "Will you come with me?" he asked her.

Jessica didn't hesitate for a second. She scooped up her evening bag from the leather chair and rushed over to take his hand. "Let's go!" she urged.

Cameron still didn't move. "You would actually leave with me?"

"We don't have time for this," Jessica warned, tugging on his arm.

"Let me get this straight," he said. "You would duck out of here with me—even if it means giving up a fancy dinner party with the top man at Mode?"

Jessica planted a swift kiss on his lips. "You're the one I want to have dinner with," she told him. "I might even have enough money in my bag to treat you to a pizza."

Cameron gazed into her eyes. "Thanks, Jessica. Maybe some other time." Then he started laughing and wrapped his arms around her.

Jessica pulled herself away and stared at him. "What is so funny?" she demanded. "Are you intentionally trying to get yourself in trouble with Mr. McGee?"

"It wouldn't be the first time," Cameron muttered wryly. He tucked a lock of Jessica's hair behind her ear and smiled tenderly. "Let me introduce myself . . . I'm Cameron McGee."

Elizabeth sat at her desk, staring at her computer screen. She'd been trying for nearly two hours to finish her "Personal Profiles" column for the *Oracle*, but her mind kept drifting off the subject. She had interviewed Aaron Dallas about his internship with the L.A. Lakers, and though he'd had lots of interesting things to say, Elizabeth was having a hard time putting any of it into coherent sentences. *Concentrate!* she mentally ordered herself.

She stiffened her fingers over the keyboard and forced her attention back to her work. "'The Lakers team is like a family,' Aaron says. 'A *real* family—with sibling rivalry and a weird uncle,'" she began writing.

An image of Todd's face floated into her mind. Jessica had told her that Simone was back with Quentin. *Does Todd still have feelings for her?* Elizabeth wondered.

She thought back to the last time she'd seen Todd, when she'd caught a glimpse of him in the Mode building after Leona had been arrested. *If he hadn't gone to the police, Leona might still be free,* she realized.

Elizabeth sighed deeply. She knew she'd be

forever grateful to Todd for his help, especially during that horrible episode on the mountain road. . . .

"Not again!" Elizabeth shrieked as she realized she'd slipped back into her daydreams. She banged her fist on the desk, rattling the pencils and paper clips that were scattered across it.

Elizabeth got up and began pacing across her bedroom. For the past few days she'd tried almost frantically to jump back into her old routine at Sweet Valley High—volunteering to do extra assignments for the *Oracle*, signing up to tutor students who were having difficulties in English class, hanging out at the Dairi Burger with Enid and Maria, going to movies, the beach. . . .

But nothing seemed *right* to her anymore. It was as if her world had been skewed a few degrees, throwing everything off-balance.

Elizabeth plopped down on her bed and stared at the ceiling. She was pleased with the way things had turned out at *Flair*. Leona was in jail, Reggie and Gordon were dating, and Elizabeth had received the credit she deserved for "Free Style" and had been promised a summer job in the editorial department if she wanted it.

But none of those things could fill the gaping hole in Elizabeth's heart. Tears pooled in her eyes, spilling down the sides of her face. *I miss Todd,* she silently admitted.

Suddenly Elizabeth heard music coming from outside her window. She recognized the Jamie

Peters ballad immediately. She and Todd had danced to it the night they'd pledged their love to each other. Elizabeth swallowed against the thickening lump in her throat. Hearing the song now made her feel as if she might drown in a flood of her own emotions.

Elizabeth sat up, her heart thumping wildly. *It could only be Todd,* she thought, laughing as tears streamed down her face. She grabbed a wad of tissues from the box on her nightstand and rushed across the room. She held her breath as she pushed aside her curtains and peered outside.

Todd was standing under her window, holding a portable CD player. He had a serious but hopeful expression on his face, as if he had something important on his mind. . . . *Like maybe our relationship,* Elizabeth thought longingly.

A feeling of glorious happiness leaped in her heart. She opened the window and leaned out. "Excuse me, mister," she called to him jokingly. "I don't seem to have any loose change right now—but I do have lots of stuff in my desk drawer . . . would you mind if I tipped you in paper clips?"

Todd barely cracked a smile as he continued gazing up at her with an intense look in his eyes. "Elizabeth, will you take me back?"

Elizabeth blinked back her happy tears. "I don't know," she gently teased. "I might say yes . . . if you can make it up to my window."

Todd flashed her a huge grin and darted around

the corner of the house. He came back carrying a tall ladder. "No problem," he said.

Elizabeth laughed heartily. A sense of peace and rightness came over her. She and Todd shared something almost magical, something much more important than any job. "By the way," she called down to him. "I love you."

Todd smiled brightly. "In that case I'd better hurry."

"You do that," Elizabeth replied. After being apart for so long, she couldn't wait another minute to feel Todd's arms around her again, his lips on hers. . . .

Then suddenly he was there, crawling into her room. He stood for a moment in front of the window, the curtains fluttering at his sides. Elizabeth gazed at him, taking in the sight of him standing so close . . . finally.

They moved toward each other, and at last she was in his arms. She wrapped her arms around his neck and closed her eyes, letting the glorious moment seep into her heart. "Elizabeth, I'm so sorry . . . tell me you forgive me," Todd whispered into her ear.

Tears flowed from her eyes as Elizabeth looked into his. "I do," she sobbed. Then their lips met in a deep, searing kiss.

Jessica sighed contentedly as she snuggled closer to Cameron on the couch in Mr. McGee's study. "This is the best dinner party I've ever been invited to," she murmured.

Cameron chuckled softly. "I think they started eating without us. But if you're hungry, I can find something for us in the kitchen."

"No way," she countered with mock indignation. "I've been agonizing for days over whether or not I'd ever see you again." She tightened her arms around him and flashed him a saucy grin. "Now that I've got you, I'm not letting you out of my sight."

Cameron gently stroked the side of her face with his fingertips. "Jessica, I'm sorry it took me so long to finally come to my senses. I must've picked up the phone to call you at least a hundred times— but I was afraid you'd hang up on me."

Jessica gaped at him. "Why would I do that?"

"It seemed whenever I was around you, I'd turn into an arrogant jerk," Cameron admitted. "When I think of some of the nasty lines that popped out of my mouth—'Too bad your insides aren't as lovely as your outside'?" He shook his head woefully. "And then that night at Spago's . . . the girl of my dreams tells me she's in love with me. And I respond with a don't-call-us-we'll-call-you brush-off. I think my only excuse is that I was jealous—and that's a new experience for me."

Jessica's heart melted at the sorrowful expression in his sexy brown eyes. "We've hurt each other a lot. I say it's time to kiss and make up," she said, pressing her lips against his. Cameron deepened the kiss, sending delicious tingles up and down Jessica's spine.

When the kiss ended, Jessica leaned back so that she could look at Cameron directly. "Now it's time for me to apologize," she said. "I'm sorry that I didn't stop seeing Quentin after I fell in love with you. But I never cared two cents for him, and that's the truth."

Cameron brushed his lips across hers. "I know. I was in the studio Monday morning."

Jessica grimaced, remembering her ugly scene with Quentin and Simone. "You heard it?"

"I heard it," he replied. "I was up in the executive suite when all that trouble broke out with your sister and Leona Peirson. Then someone happened to mention that you were also in the building." Cameron paused. "I wanted to see you again and figured the most likely place to find you would be in the photography studio."

Jessica took a deep breath and let it out slowly. "So how much of the fireworks display did you manage to catch?"

"Every word," he answered.

"Dazzling, wasn't it?" Jessica groaned.

Cameron rolled his eyes. "Quentin and Simone," he muttered. "What a pair . . . I wonder what they're saying now that they've seen the blue pages."

Jessica giggled. "I'm sure it's something loud

and vicious. But how did my photos get into the layout?" she asked. "I thought Quentin had the last word."

Cameron shook his head. "He only thinks he does. The final decisions are made by the executive board—and as a vice president of the company, I chose your photos for the layout."

Jessica digested that bit of information. "So not only are you the owner's son—you're also a *vice president?* Gee, that's a nice promotion for a mail-room clerk," she teased. "But I suppose you'll have to give up your job waiting tables at Spago's."

Cameron laughed. "We have a lot of misunder-standings to unravel, don't we?"

"Let's start with why you were working in the mail room as Mr. Smith," Jessica suggested.

"As a brand-new vice president, I wanted to get a feel for the company from the inside," Cameron explained. "I wasn't satisfied to do the usual execu-tive tour where you go around to all the different departments, shaking hands, pausing for an occa-sional ten-second conversation if you're not run-ning behind schedule. . . . I wanted to learn how things ran on a day-to-day basis, but I wouldn't have been able to work alongside our employees if everyone knew I was the owner's son. So I made up a fake name."

"No *wonder* I wasn't able to find you in the phone book," Jessica said. "That was very sneaky of you."

Cameron wrapped his arms around her. "I wanted to tell you the truth, Jessica. But after I realized how I felt about you, it became important for me to know that you care about *me*, not my money."

Jessica looked into his eyes. "And do you know it now?" she whispered.

"Absolutely," he replied, moving in for a long, burning kiss.

I've sure lucked out, Jessica thought happily. Not only had she gotten the guy of her dreams but *also* someone who could help her with her career. . . .

What a great internship! she silently cheered. And then she was lost in the warmth of Cameron's passionate kiss.

Next, travel with Jessica and Elizabeth to Château d'Amour Inconnu, a French castle by the sea, for a summer of royalty and romance. Don't miss **Once Upon a Time,** *the first book in an enchanting three-part miniseries— coming soon. It's a fairy tale come true!*

Bantam Books in the Sweet Valley High series
Ask your bookseller for the books you have missed

SIGN UP FOR THE SWEET VALLEY HIGH® FAN CLUB!

Hey, girls! Get all the gossip on Sweet Valley High's® most popular teenagers when you join our fantastic Fan Club! As a member, you'll get all of this really cool stuff:

- Membership Card with your own personal Fan Club ID number
- A Sweet Valley High® Secret Treasure Box
- Sweet Valley High® Stationery
- Official Fan Club Pencil (for secret note writing!)
- Three Bookmarks
- A "Members Only" Door Hanger
- Two Skeins of J. & P. Coats® Embroidery Floss with flower barrette instruction leaflet
- Two editions of *The Oracle* newsletter
- Plus exclusive Sweet Valley High® product offers, special savings, contests, and much more!

Be the first to find out what Jessica & Elizabeth Wakefield are up to by joining the Sweet Valley High® Fan Club for the one-year membership fee of only $6.25 each for U.S. residents, $8.25 for Canadian residents (U.S. currency). Includes shipping & handling.

Send a check or money order (do not send cash) made payable to "Sweet Valley High® Fan Club" along with this form to:

SWEET VALLEY HIGH® FAN CLUB, BOX 3919-B, SCHAUMBURG, IL 60168-3919

NAME _____
(Please print clearly)

ADDRESS _____

CITY_____ STATE _____ ZIP_____
(Required)

AGE _____ BIRTHDAY_____ / _____ / _____